Little JOE

by SANDRA NEIL WALLACE
illustrated by Mark Elliott

Alfred A. Knopf
New York

THIS IS A BORZOI BOOK PUBLISHED BY ALFRED A. KNOPF

Grateful acknowledgment is made to Storey Publishing, LLC, for permission to reprint the endpaper illustration by Elayne Sears, copyright © by Elayne Sears.

Visit us on the Web! www.randomhouse.com/kids

Educators and librarians, for a variety of teaching tools, visit us at
www.randomhouse.com/teachers

Library of Congress Cataloging-in-Publication Data
Wallace, Sandra Neil.
Little Joe / by Sandra Neil Wallace. — 1st ed.
p. cm.
Summary: Nine-year-old Eli raises his first bull calf and looks forward to showing it at the county fair.
ISBN 978-0-375-86097-3 (trade) — ISBN 978-0-375-96097-0 (lib. bdg.) —
ISBN 978-0-375-89707-8 (e-book)
[1. Bulls—Fiction. 2. Farm life—Fiction. 3. Country life—Fiction.] I. Title.
PZ7.W15879Li 2010
[Fic]—dc20
2009042362

The text of this book is set in 12-point Century Book.

Printed in the United States of America
August 2010
10 9 8 7 6 5 4 3 2 1
First Edition

To my father, John Neil,
who comes from a farming family,
and my oma, Anna Koenig, who lost her farm to war.
Like Eli's grandpa, she encouraged me to roam.

Chapter One

⚜

A Special Delivery

Little Joe came out on Christmas Eve, when he wasn't supposed to. Larger than most and trembly, with only Eli there and Grandpa. Pa had gone to fetch the in-laws and some ice cream to go with the pies.

"Fancy's been like this for over an hour, son," Grandpa said to Eli, stroking Fancy's matted hair. "She's gonna need some help with this one."

A nervous hen fluttered a wing, then clucked. One of the barn cats purred. But their movements were blurred by the darkness. All Eli could see in the barn was what stirred beneath the pen's only lightbulb: two little black hooves no bigger than Eli's wrists, peeking out of Fancy.

Then a head, black and furry and shiny, with two slits for eyes shut tight.

Eli stared at the hooves just dangling there. He'd seen calves being born before—even twins last year, back when he was eight. But they were little Holstein heifers, not Angus like this one. And they'd come out right away, splashing slick as a waterslide onto the bedding and bawling for their mama.

"Push against Fancy's side," Grandpa told Eli. Grandpa took hold of the tiny hooves and pulled while Eli pushed against Fancy. But the calf stayed put.

"Looks like you're gonna have to pull on a hoof with me, Eli, just like you would a wishbone. You pull thataway and I'll pull this way," Grandpa said. "Now make a wish and when I holler three . . . *pull!* On a count o' three. One . . ."

Eli clenched his teeth, grabbed hold of a hoof and shut his eyes tight as he could.

"Two . . ."

Then he wished for the calf to come out right.

"Three!"

Eli yanked on the hoof. Grandpa tugged hard on the other. Then Eli heard a plop and the rustling of straw.

"You can open your eyes now," Grandpa said, grinning. "It's a fine bull calf, Eli."

Lying on the straw bed was a shimmering black clump

of a calf. Perfectly shaped and nearly as long as Eli, he'd come out right and big.

"Your pa says this one's yours," Grandpa said.

"Pa said so?" Eli looked down at the newborn and fought back a smile. His own calf! And Pa was giving it to him.

Grandpa stopped smiling. He got down on his knees again and stroked the bull calf's side. Its eyes were closed and it wasn't moving. Not like the heifers. The heifers moved, Eli remembered. The heifers tried to get up, raise their heads. The heifers tried to do something—anything— to get a feel for the outside. This one did nothing.

"He's not breathing." Grandpa knelt closer and felt the calf's nose. "It's too late to get Doc Rutledge. Breathe into this nostril while I close off the other. *Now*, Eli!"

Eli grabbed hold of the bull calf's head, took a deep breath and blew into the shiny gray nostril, hard as he could. The nostril was slippery cold, and Eli was sure it hadn't moved.

"Again!" Grandpa shouted as he felt for the calf's heart. "And through the mouth, too."

Eli drew in another deep breath and forced it into the gray nostril. This time he pressed his lips against the calf's mouth, too, blowing through a tiny row of baby teeth.

"Keep going!" Grandpa yelled.

Lying on the straw bed was a shimmering black clump of a calf.
Perfectly shaped and nearly as long as Eli, he'd come out right and big.

There was pounding in Eli's ears now. He was sweating and sure his face must be red as a summer radish. His hands had gone all shaky, too. Eli worried they might not be any good to the calf. *His calf*. Still, he took another gulp of air and fed it into the bull calf's nose.

"He's got a heartbeat," Grandpa said.

The bull calf coughed and sputtered, then spit up a big wad of goo into Eli's face.

Eli didn't know what to do, so he swiped at the goo and just sat there, leaning against the wall of the pen until the coolness came back to him. Grandpa always said those stone walls held history and the stories of all the Stegner seasons. That they soaked up the cold and kept it there, year-round, soothing you in summer and forcing you awake in winter to get your chores done. Eli couldn't imagine going to sleep now. He shivered as the stone's cold bore through his chore coat.

"Feel the heart, Eli." Grandpa took Eli's hand and placed it under the calf's left foreleg, below the rib cage. The heart was warm and restless. It kept fluttering, just like the monarch butterfly Eli'd cupped in his hands last spring.

"It's beating because of you, Eli. You got it goin'!" Grandpa smiled and looked at Fancy. "Come, Mama," he called. Fancy got up, turned around and smelled her calf for the first time.

"Better wipe that slobber off your face unless you want Fancy to give you a lickin', too," Grandpa teased. "Now go get her some water, son."

Eli grabbed the water bucket and ran to the hose fast as he could. He thought about taking that hose and hauling it right over to Fancy, but decided to stand and wait for the bucket to fill. He'd forgotten it was snowing. That it was Christmas Eve. Eli pawed at the snowdrift that had found its way into the barn below the old stanchions. He ran a frozen clump of it down the side of his face where the goo was. Then he carted the bucket over to the calving pen, trying not to spill too much.

When Eli got back, Grandpa was putting a piece of straw up the little calf's nose to make it sneeze. It sneezed.

Eli laughed. "My bull calf sneezed!"

"Just checking his breathing, son."

It sneezed again.

"Gave us quite a scare, didn't he?" Grandpa slid his hands across the bull calf's loin, past the rump, then stopped to massage its hindquarters. "You know, I was bigger than most, too, when I was born, oh, about a hundred years ago."

"Grandpa, you're not *that* old," Eli said.

"What you gonna name him, son? He's sired by Apple Wood, and if he's anything like his daddy, he'll be worth keeping as a bull. But you can call him anything you want to, on account he's all yours."

The bull calf raised its head, sniffed at the pen and mooed.

"Pretty soon you'll know his moo, Eli, and he'll get familiar with your voice—how you smell. Now don't go washing that chore coat. The more it's got the scent of him on it, the better. Once a calf trusts you, it can be gentled."

The barn seemed different to Eli now that it had new life in it. There was sneezing and bleating and the rush of warm milk. All because there was something to fuss over.

"Merry Christmas, everybody!" Hannah burst into the barn out of breath, with her puffy coat undone and her jeans halfway tucked into pink cowboy boots. "Ma said if you're in here this long, there must be . . . Ah!" Hannah gasped. "There *is* a calf being born!" She rushed right up to the little bull calf. "Oh, look how cute it is."

"Careful, Hannah," Grandpa warned. "This here's Eli's bull calf, and your big brother's just about to name him."

"Can I touch him, Eli?" Hannah pleaded. "Oh, can I? Please, please!"

Eli nodded.

"How 'bout Kris Kringle!" Hannah gushed, rubbing the curly knot of hair on the bull calf's forehead. "Since it's

Christmas Eve and all. Santa Claus seems too . . . babyish. But Kris Kringle, that sounds royal."

"Don't you want Santa Claus to come visit tonight?" Grandpa asked.

"Yes, but I'd rather call him Kris Kringle." Hannah puckered out her lower lip. "That's who I wrote to, anyway, about the trampoline I wished for. *If* it happens to go on sale. Plus, the Misty Mate rabbit cooler, the pony beads and the unicorn-mane-braiding kit—either/or."

Eli stroked the top of Fancy's tail, ignoring Hannah and thinking of a name instead.

"Grandpa, do you think Kris Kringle knows anything about unicorns?" Hannah asked. "Since he's only got reindeer?"

Both Grandpa and Eli knew whenever Hannah got this way, the best thing to do was just let her go.

"I know," Hannah said. "How about Jesus! He was born tonight, too. Who wouldn't be impressed with the name Jesus?"

Grandpa said he didn't think calling the bull calf Jesus and having it hollered out over the loudspeaker above the fairgrounds would help Eli in the show ring much.

"Remember how you get to name all your bunnies whenever Snow White has a litter?" Grandpa reminded her.

Hannah nodded and tied the fuzzy scarf around her neck into a bow.

"Now go inside and tell your ma there's a calf out here. And that we'll be inside soon for dessert."

"Hey-Ma-there's-a-calf-out-here!" Hannah yelled as she headed for the house.

"How about Joe?" Eli said. "That's your name. Huh, Grandpa?"

Grandpa's nose turned red. "Well, he *is* big. . . ."

The calf was so big, Grandpa said he just *had* to put "little" in front of Joe. Said he'd like to see the look on all the people's faces when they heard his name announced at the County Fair and out walked the biggest little bull calf they'd ever seen. Then the bidding would start and they'd all be giddy to get a piece of Little Joe.

"You'll make good money off this calf," Grandpa said. "Once he wins the blue ribbon. It's a Stegner tradition."

Fancy finished licking Little Joe clean, then her and Old Gert started doing what mother cows do, hiding Little Joe by covering him up with so much straw and hay and mud that only they could find him.

When Eli came back to the barn after pie and ice cream, his heart crept into his throat. He couldn't see Little Joe anywhere. He pulled up the switch on Fancy's tail and got down in the straw on his hands and knees, poking around Old Gertie's legs.

The cows got so bothered they walked right over to

the heap where Little Joe was. Eli felt so relieved to uncover him, he gave them all more water and took a drink, too.

The wind groaned in the rafters above. It lingered high in the hay mow, causing the mice to scatter. Eli looked up and eyed the lightbulb flickering. At their end of the barn, Ma's broody hens cooed faintly. They knew something was different.

Fancy gave her calf a nudge, and in no time he was up on his wobbly legs. Trembling on all fours, he looked up at Eli with the biggest blue eyes Eli had ever seen. Blinking back wonder, Little Joe leaned and swayed in between Fancy and Old Gert until he gave up and flopped back down to give it a rest.

Grandpa walked into the birthing pen with a little brown jar and some rubber gloves. "Now it's important that you take care of the navel." He took hold of the brown stringy cord still hanging from Little Joe's navel and dipped the end into the jar.

Little Joe's belly shivered as his navel cord got dunked.

"It's important that it doesn't get infected. The cord'll fall off in a few days, but you still need to rub the navel with iodine, Eli. So Little Joe won't have any problems."

Eli'd make sure nothing would happen to that navel. That nothing would happen to Little Joe. His first calf. The scare was over and done with. He'd gotten Little Joe to breathe. Now the calf was safe under Fancy, sucking on warm milk. *Fancy deserves some grain for all this*, Eli thought. *And a good rest.*

Carefully, Eli took the brown jar and the rubber gloves from Grandpa and put them back in the medicine cabinet hanging in the tack room. Then he spotted the pictures above the feed bin. There was Grandpa and Pa, not much older than Eli, smiling with their milkers at the County Fair. Grandpa's photo was in black and white, but Eli knew the ribbon was blue—FIRST PLACE it said along the shiny side of the satin. Pa's picture with his grand champion was in color and he was kind of smiling, sort of. That was smiling for Pa—pressing both lips together tight.

Eli had a checked shirt just like the one in Pa's picture. Maybe he'd wear it to the fair next year when he'd show Little Joe. Eli would be the first Stegner in the ring with a beef bull calf, now that they weren't a milking operation anymore. "No money in milkers" is what Pa had said. He'd sold every one of the dairy cows last year, except Old Gert. So Eli'd be starting a new tradition.

Eli clutched the scoop and dug it deep into the feed bin. He poured the golden kernels into the red rubber tub and ran with it to give to Fancy. She looked tired and a little dazed. Her eyes were glassy, too; still, she took the feed. Eli scratched the back of her ears. Then he whispered,

"Merry Christmas, Fancy," in one. This was the best Christmas present he'd ever had. Better than the John Deere cast-iron tractor he'd gotten two Christmases ago. Or the junior bow and arrow set from last year.

Eli reached out and touched Little Joe for the first time without being scared. Little Joe's spotted gray muzzle was wet with milk and warm as a hot-water bottle, only softer and loaded with whiskers. Eli didn't even care if he got a fishing rod from Kris Kringle or Santa Claus this year. He'd just gotten the best present ever. More than he could have imagined. He'd gotten Little Joe.

"You can't stay here all night, son."

Eli didn't know how long Pa'd been standing there, scratching his head with his cap still on it.

"Is he really mine, Pa?"

"Isn't that what Grandpa said?"

"Yeah." Eli nodded. "I named him Little Joe."

Pa took off the Carhartt coat he'd gotten for Christmas last year and hung it over Eli's shoulders. "You'd better get to bed or Santa Claus might not show."

"It's Kris Kringle," Eli murmured.

"Says who?"

"Hannah. That's who she wrote to this year."

Chapter Two

Tattoo Day

Snow had made the farm so quiet Eli couldn't hear the morning coming. But he could feel it: the frosty chill of his breath against a bare elbow as he turned over and remembered he had a bull calf, just four days old. It was barely light out. The windowpanes were still crusted over with ice. Scratching them to get a good look outside would only wake up Hannah next door. Besides, he knew the barn was knee-deep in snow. Had been since Christmas. Eli's window faced the barn's McIntosh red shingles. If he sat straight and balled up three pillows just right, Eli could usually catch sight of the silver-tipped weather vane and the SWEPT in WINDSWEPT FARMS. Not today, though.

Just a cloudy mess that looked like chicken feet scratches running up and down the glass.

Eli felt a draft shoot up his back. He tugged at the comforter. It wouldn't budge but gave a familiar grumble. Taking the flashlight from under his pillow, he aimed it at the foot of the bed, where the dog lay. Tater had snuck in trying to get warm and was hogging all the covers. Tater opened one eye and followed the beam for a bit as it traced his potato-colored fur. But he soon lost interest and was snoring by the time Eli turned off the switch.

Eli crept out of bed and winced as his bare feet touched the floor. He wondered if Little Joe was warm enough in the maternity pen. Its windows would be frosted over, too. Reaching under the bed for yesterday's socks, Eli snuck out as quiet as he could.

Icy pellets of snow began to smatter against the window between Eli's and Hannah's rooms. It looked over the pastures where Little Joe would be tasting timothy and white clover in a few months. Now they were bloated with snow and dotted by deer tracks crisscrossing the fence lines.

Hannah would be sore he hadn't woke her up. But she'd just spook Little Joe anyway and take over with all her talking. Besides, Eli liked being the only one in the barn.

Eli's boots broke through a crunchy layer of snow as

he cut a path to the barn. He didn't mind getting up so early winter mornings, now that he had Little Joe. But he wished he'd taken the time to put liners in his chore boots. His toes felt prickly and his Steelers cap was no match for the sleet.

The market steers'll take shelter under the tin roof next to the corral, Eli thought. They'd already been weaned off their mothers when Pa bought them in the fall. They didn't get warm milk like Little Joe.

Must be twenty below with the wind, Eli figured. He saw the ax leaning heavy against the barn. He knew the first thing he should do was take it and chop the ice off the water trough the steers drank from. But the trough was a quarter mile away and all Eli could think about was his bull calf. *I'll make sure to fork out more hay and scatter it around the herd*, he thought, eyeing the barn door.

Eli sucked in his breath and slid the door open. He leaned back, feeling for the stone step with his foot as he always did before putting his full weight on it. Then he descended several feet into the world inside the barn. Darkness surrounded him, cave-like and moist. He'd welcomed that dampness in summer, when it was a soothing wetness. Now it was stone-cold and icicle-tingly. Eli's pulse quickened as he made his way deeper, guided by the gullies cut into the cement floor.

It took a few blinks before Eli could take in the dimness. What lay inside revealed itself in pieces. First, it was the shape of things. Two wooden arms of a wheelbarrow splayed sideways against a whitewashed post. Next, the jagged teeth of barbed wire. Piercing the air in circles, it glinted silver around spools as high as Eli's waist. Then finally, movement. Eli spotted a smoky curl, hairy and soft. It wove through his legs in a quivering tickle. The curl turned serious, into a shove only a barn cat could give. A shove that nearly toppled Eli over until he leaned down and stroked it.

The cat purred and followed Eli as far as the pen, where they heard chewing.

Every time Eli entered the barn this early, he thought he'd wake up the animals, but it never worked out that way. They were always up before anybody else. Spider, the youngest of the tabby barn cats, was up, too, balancing on top of the stanchion wall. It couldn't have been more than an inch wide, which suited Spider just fine. Spider could climb most anything a real spider could, the thinner the better. She licked the back of a mackerel-striped paw, peered over Little Joe in the maternity pen and mewed.

"He's your calf, too, huh, Spider?" Eli'd seen Spider nuzzled up against Little Joe's stomach yesterday afternoon. Eli wished he could get that close. He stretched out his arm and made a bridge across the stanchion, but Spider didn't need it. She jumped onto Eli's shoulder, clear.

Eli rubbed his hands together to find some heat. The barn wasn't much warmer than outside and it was dark. He couldn't reach the lightbulb on the low beam yet, and the switch had been broke for years.

Little Joe shook his ears and hid behind Fancy as Eli unlocked the latch and came into the pen with a bucket of grain.

Keep humming, Eli remembered Grandpa saying. *And pretend not to look.* It had been four days since Little Joe was born, and Eli worked on gentling him. Still, Little Joe snuck behind his mama no matter how slowly Eli slid the pitchfork into the straw to scoop up the manure. Little Joe would lower his neck, thick and fuzzy as a bear cub, and peek at Eli through Fancy's legs. And no matter what Eli hummed, tossing the clumps into a wheelbarrow, Little Joe wouldn't take water from the bucket Eli'd freshened until after Eli left.

Maybe he'd like other songs besides Christmas carols, Eli thought. Christmas was over, but it was still Christmas-cold. Eli caught sight of his breath whenever he stopped humming. All he could think of to hum was Grandpa's favorite—the "Pennsylvania Polka." So he started humming that.

Little Joe's ears pricked up.

Eli edged closer and Fancy mooed. He gave her some grain and wondered why Pa had put the halter on her. She and Little Joe wouldn't be grazing for months and didn't need to be led.

Little Joe head-butted Fancy's water bucket. It lay on its side, the top frozen over. Fumbling in his pockets for some gloves, Eli found the pair with the holes in them. He knelt and broke up the icy layer with his bare fingers. Then he felt a nudge. Before he knew it, he was flat on his face in the straw, with a hand in the icy bucket of water.

"Hey, cut it out!" Eli said. Little Joe had nudged him hard and was sucking on Eli's wet fingers.

Eli pulled his fingers free, but Little Joe gripped Eli's wrist with his tongue.

"Hey—I ain't no blade of grass." Eli laughed. Little Joe's tongue was strong as a suction cup and felt like fine-grit sandpaper against Eli's skin. It was different from a Holstein tongue. Little Joe's was black on top, bubble gum pink underneath and bent on keeping hold of Eli.

"You're really mine, aren't you?" The thought burst into Eli's head straightaway and stood there tingling, finally taking hold. He reached with his other hand and stroked the stray wisps of hair sprouting up between Little Joe's ears. Then he leaned closer and smelled his calf. He knew he'd never forget that smell. It was sweet and fresh—a mixture of earth after rain, just-boiled milk and the fleshy parts of Tater's ears.

"Maybe you're ready to be gentled after all, huh, boy?"

Little Joe sneezed, flashing his bottom teeth.

"What's so funny?" Hannah asked, peering over the pen door.

"Aren't you supposed to be helping Ma?" Eli got up slowly and brushed the straw from his jeans.

"I have time." Hannah smiled. "The hair dye Ma's mixing hasn't turned purple yet." She gripped a rail and swung one leg over the pen wall.

"Ah, don't come in, Hannah." Eli scowled. "You'll scare off Little Joe."

"No I won't. I know how to be careful."

"You got to be quiet as Spider when you climb over, or he'll skitter away."

Hannah hoisted the other leg over, then jumped.

Eli watched his bull calf dart behind Fancy. "I don't go chasing your rabbits away, do I?" he moaned.

"Maybe he likes to hide." Hannah squatted on the butt ends of her pink boots and looked at Little Joe skittering under Fancy's legs. "My bunnies do. They like being chased, too." Hannah inched closer. "Oh, Eli, his eyes are bigger than most. That means he's smart. Snow White's are the size of rubies and she knew how to pose right away."

Hannah stood up and stuck her face into a cobweb. It clung to her chin, thick as maple sap. "Get it off me, Eli!" she shrieked.

Eli laughed and let Hannah claw at the dangling web before scraping it off with his thumb.

Eli'd studied those cobwebs sometimes while doing his farm chores. He noticed they weren't thin and silky like the willowy ones you'd find in a house; barn cobwebs were thick and as solidly wound as string. They hung in sagging clumps fat as spitballs and just as white, weaving their way around anything with corners.

"There's no cobwebs at Sassy Clippers," Hannah sniffed, thrusting a boot back over the pen wall. "I'm going to help Ma."

The sun was up by now and spilling into the windows. It shone through Little Joe's tail, soft and downy at the tips and not yet tangled up or dirty. It shone through the pink parts between the ridges of Little Joe's ears when he bobbed up from his mama to see if Eli was still there.

As soon as Eli looked at those ears, he realized what today was—tattoo day. He suspected Little Joe wouldn't like it one bit.

Eli'd seen plenty of cattle being tagged—Pa did it every year—but you didn't have to tattoo milkers, on account of they weren't certified Angus beef. And tagging was different from tattooing, Grandpa told him. Tagging was like getting your ears pierced.

The smell of disinfectant met Eli's nose before he saw Pa coming. Then Pa rounded the corner, screwed on the lightbulb and placed a silver pan swirling with alcohol on a bale of alfalfa next to the corral.

"Do we keep him in the pen?" Eli asked.

"Nah." Pa pulled out the tattoo kit from under his arm. "Too little for that. He'd wrestle free in no time once we'd take hold of his head."

Pa had the kit open. He gripped the tattoo pliers, pressing hard on the handles. Then he dunked some metal digits into the silver pan. They clinked and bubbled as they went in. Eli could see that their points were made of tiny needles.

"But he's not even halter-broke," Eli said. "How you gonna get him out?"

In four strides Pa had the corral gate open. Now he was clipping a lead strap onto Fancy. Of course Little Joe would follow. He buried his forehead behind her hock and headed for the gate, too.

"Shouldn't we wait for Grandpa?" Eli asked, watching their hooves clip the cement floor as he tried to keep up. "He could hold down Little Joe so's he could stay right in the pen."

"I'm at the sawmill today." Pa led Fancy through the

shiny blue work chute and into the lot where all the steers were. "Besides, I can do it myself."

Little Joe followed Fancy toward the lot, but as soon as his shoulders reached the head gate, Pa squeezed it shut, locking Little Joe in the chute.

. When it sank in that he'd been caught, the bull calf jerked his head back, but the chute only had a few inches to give.

"Take this sponge and wipe the earlobes with it, Eli, to get the wax off E-1's skin."

"Who's E-1?" The sleet had started up again and pounded down on Little Joe's poll. Eli stared at the knotty lump between the calf's ears.

"Your bull calf." Pa snapped the tattoo digits onto the pliers.

"You mean Little Joe?"

Little Joe snorted and showed the whites of his eyes. His mouth began to froth up and he started bawling.

"He's E-1 to me, son. If you're wise, he would be to you, too. No use naming something that's gonna get eaten."

Little Joe's ears kept flicking as Eli rubbed them with the soggy sponge.

"*E* stands for 'Eli,' " Pa said, testing the tattoo on a piece of paper. "Then *one*, 'cause it's your first show animal. Now hand me that tube of green paste."

Little Joe kept fighting the chute, banging against its sides to get free and bawling each time he couldn't.

Satisfied the tattoo had come out right on paper, Pa rubbed his fingers full of green ink. "Best to think of the calf as a number, boy. You'll just have to part with it next fall."

Spider hopped onto the railing and hissed.

The wind had changed course. The sleet was going in all directions now. Eli brushed an icy drip from his Steelers cap and eyed Pa. "What about all them dairy cows you had, Pa, right since you were little? What'd you call them?"

"C-1 through 949. And number 949—the very last one—was just plain miserable."

Eli looked over to the lot at the steers herded up and facing them. Slick with sleet and munching on hay, the crossbreds were pinned with green tags dangling from their ears. Eli knew that the numbers and letters written in black marker had been done by Pa.

He caught sight of Fancy and Old Gert.

"Then why's Old Gert called 'Old Gert' and Fancy 'Fancy'?" Eli wanted to know.

"Gert belonged to Grandma, and Fancy's the cow your grandpa bought us to get this beef operation started."

But Eli didn't quite remember it that way. To him, Gert

was as much Pa's as Grandma's. Hadn't Pa stayed up all night with Old Gert, back when she was still a milker and carrying twins? Maybe Pa was still sore about selling his dairy cows. He'd moped around that first afternoon come milking time last spring, not knowing what to do. Now he worked over at the sawmill while Ma cut hair in the old milk house.

"Go rub your hands with alcohol and get the sponge. There's bound to be some blood," Pa said.

Pa smeared the ink paste into Little Joe's ears with his fingers. Then he put the jaws of the tattoo pliers against a lobe and clamped down.

Eli couldn't swallow. Couldn't look. Instead, he eyed Little Joe's hooves and saw the drops of blood begin to color the snow. He felt helpless. Helpless as Little Joe. The bull calf thrashed against the chute. Eli could hear the metal rattling, see the hooves tramping on the snow. But soon the bawling drowned out everything.

"Rub the paste in that ear with your thumb, Eli, till all the bleeding's stopped."

Eli did what he was told and felt the ridges in the calf's ear with his thumb. He knew Little Joe must be sore at him. And afraid of Pa. How would Eli gentle Little Joe now?

"It takes a while to break 'em down, but they get to know the score soon enough," Pa explained. "They don't win."

Hannah came out from the barn all happy. "I've come to help," she shouted. "Ma's cutting Mrs. Motichka's hair and won't let me listen."

"Oh no." Pa put down the pliers and shooed Hannah away.

"How come Little Joe's crying so much?" she asked.

"Not now, Hannah." Pa stood square in front of the calf.

"But what are you doing? Ma says I'm old enough to—" Hannah stopped talking when she saw the blood.

"Bet you don't want to get your ears pierced now, huh, Hannah?" Eli knew it was mean, but he was mad. Pa had made Little Joe afraid. He'd never get Little Joe to trust him. He'd think this was all Eli's fault.

Hannah put her hands to her mouth and screamed.

"The blood should taper off soon," Pa said. But Hannah had already fled into the barn.

"The hard part's over, Eli." Pa closed up the tattoo kit and dipped his fingers in the disinfectant. "We can tag E-1 if you want to, but it can get in the way of the show halter."

Eli shook his head, so Pa went over to the lot and got Fancy.

"There's a difference between them and you, Eli." Pa swung the chute open and Little Joe staggered out, still bawling as Fancy licked his hide.

"You're in charge," Pa explained. "That's what keeps 'em afraid."

Fancy tucked the bull calf close behind her rib as Pa shooed them into the barn. Eli wanted to follow, to be with them, but what would Pa think? Instead, he stood still.

"Remember that when you take the rope halter to it, Eli. You can't give 'em an inch. And don't ever let go."

Chapter Three

❧

Sweet & Sour

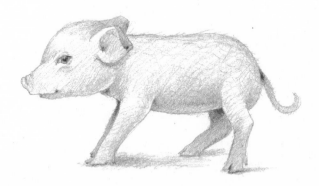

Eli didn't want to go over to Keller Tibbet's house in the first place. The gale winds of March had taken hold of the valley and hung on all week. Snowdrifts reached up to the apple branches. Even the sure-footed turkeys slid on the rock-hard snow. But Ma insisted Eli walk down and deliver the chicken potpie. She figured the Tibbets'd had their fill of junk food by now. Keller's mother was away at a horse show, and Ma'd seen Keller tossing a whole bunch of pizza boxes into a burn barrel.

"Hear your calf's got scours." Keller smirked. "Better stay clear when he fires away." Keller rested a BB gun alongside his freckled jaw and took aim at a target.

"Most every calf gets it," Eli reasoned, trying to stay

clear of the yelping Akita dogs lunging behind their kennel.

"Every baby gets the runs once in a while," Keller admitted. "Humans. Mammals." Keller put down his gun and took the dish. He balanced it on top of an empty doghouse with his bare hands. No matter how cold it got, Keller never wore gloves or a winter coat even. The first thing you noticed about Keller was those red hands, cracked and chafed up like an old farmer's. "'Cept hogs." He stabbed at a chunk of snow with his black Wolverine boots. "They could pop right out of the sow and start nibbling on nails, then guzzle it down with some beer, I swear." Keller smiled. His teeth were so big, Eli wondered if Keller had any gums and thought the top two looked like Snow White's, Hannah's rabbit. "They only get the runs at the fair when you don't expect 'em to. Right when the judge is looking."

Eli hadn't shown at the fair before, like Keller. And they weren't exactly friends. But Keller was the closest farm kid near Eli's age, so Ma kept pressing him to go visiting.

"Got one in reserve, or is the calf with diarrhea your only show animal?" Keller asked.

Eli hadn't even thought of having a backup for Little Joe. "He was born stocky," Eli said. "And he's already square right up to his rump." Eli peeled off a glove and blew on his frostbitten fingers. "My grandpa says he should do real well in his class."

Keller nodded and pulled out his jackknife. "This pie goes right in my fridge in the hog barn." He cut through the foil and sniffed. "No sharing."

Eli heard squealing and caught sight of a mess of hogs in Keller's pen. A sow, candy pink and panting, looked down at her empty feed tub and yawned. Eli wondered if she was the pig Keller showed at the fair last year—the sow who fell asleep in the middle of the show ring and didn't wake up till the class was over.

Keller held the chicken potpie away from the groveling hogs, hoisting it above his head, which was high. More than a foot taller than Eli, Keller was the only near six-footer in fourth grade. Eli knew Keller'd repeated Mrs. MacFarland's class before, at least once. And he figured Keller would be six foot for sure if he let his hair grow. But Keller was always coming around the house for a trim. Ma said he could have any haircut for free.

"Careful. Watermelon's a biter," Keller warned. Eli watched for any sniveling, open mouths and tried not to step on the feed tubs. They'd been turned over by Keller's crop of Sour Patch hogs—a bunch of weanlings, piglets and sows who were rooting the upside-down containers into the filthy snow with their grunting snouts. Keller named all his hogs after the candy he sold on the school bus. Sour Patch were by far his best seller.

Watermelon took hold of Eli's pant leg.

"Are you taking Watermelon to the fair this year?" Eli asked, tugging hard to set his pant leg free.

"Don't know yet." Keller slapped Watermelon on the backside to get him moving and out of mischief. "Too early to tell how their hams'll fatten up by the fall."

Keller walked into the barn and pulled open a rusty refrigerator door. He took out a slice of pepperoni pizza to make room for the potpie.

Two little piglets with big pink ears and silky white faces came over. They wiggled their snouts in the air and stared up at Eli with long white eyelashes. Then they saw Keller and squealed.

"The one on the left rants up already, so he's out of the question." Keller swooped down and scooped up the other with one arm. "This one's so pink, naming her Strawberry's a no-brainer." Keller pulled out a tiny pair of clippers from his back pocket. "Needle teeth," he said, trimming the pointy tip of a fingernail-length tooth. "If you don't keep an eye on 'em, they'll cut up the sow's teats real bad and all the babies go hungry."

The piglet gazed up at Keller, who reached for a bottle

stopper and nursed the piglet with it. "It's just sugar water," Keller said. "They're so dumb 'n' ornery, they'll eat anything."

Eli smiled at Strawberry looking happy inside Keller's camouflage vest. She gripped the bottle stopper like it was her mother and made all sorts of suckling sounds.

"This one sure likes to camp out," Keller said, blushing as the piglet snuggled closer. "So when's he gonna get snipped?"

"When's *who* gonna get snipped?" Eli asked.

"Your bull calf."

Pa hadn't said anything about Little Joe getting castrated. "He's staying a bull, far as I know." But Eli couldn't be sure. Whenever the milkers had bull calves, they always got sold. Pa just kept the heifers.

Keller shook his head. "They always tell you they won't snip 'em. Then when you're not looking—like if you're asleep or you're off visiting Grandpa's—even a friend—they bring in the vet and get it done."

Eli tried not to think about it. He looked at the market swine book next to the fridge. Most of the cover had been torn off or eaten.

"It's just easier to make 'em steers," Keller said. "If all bulls stayed bulls, there'd be more cows than people and folks sure would get sick and tired of eating steaks."

Didn't Grandpa say Little Joe looked good enough to stay a bull calf? Eli thought. *That any bull sired by Apple Wood would take top dollar at the County Fair?*

"When do you start training your hogs?" Eli wanted off the subject of bulls.

"You mean showing them the cane?" Keller laughed and put down the piglet. "Giving them a real bath instead of letting them roll around in wallow water?" Keller crouched over an old sink. "The hardest part's getting them used to a hog snare so's you can shave their bellies with the electric razor," he said. "That's what this swill's for." He took the lid off a great big kettle and grinned.

Eli wrinkled up his nose. It smelled awful. Like a mish-mash of everything you weren't meant to eat—leftovers gone bad, eggshells, banana peels, fish bones, too.

"Guess I'll start training right after squirrel season, I suppose." Keller took the kettle of swill into the hog pen and righted the feed tubs with his Wolverines. "Or between coyote and bee season."

"Bee season?" Eli shook his head. He knew better than to believe Keller outright. "Never heard of one." Eli'd read in the Game Commission manual Pa kept by the phone that you could kill woodchucks and weasels anytime except Sundays and crows most weekends. But bees?

"That's when the bees get all fat and start buzzin'

around the manure heap." Keller squatted beside the wire fence of the hog pen.

"Then what do you do?" A bunch of pigs started biting each other's shoulders to get to the swill.

"I catch 'em with my bare hands." Keller reached into the sky and snatched a fistful of air. Watermelon jumped a few inches to try and take a look, then bit a few tails and got up to the swill.

"Doesn't that sting?" Eli'd stepped on a fallen hornets' nest once, chasing Tater through the grass in his bare feet. He didn't think anything could hurt so much for so long.

"Not to me," Keller said. "I'm immuned."

"But why'd you catch a bee for anyway?" Eli knew about honey, but that's what bees made, not what they were made of.

"I eat 'em. Tastes just like candy, you know. With a little fuzz on top. No different than biting into a honeycomb, only crunchier with more stuff squirting out." Keller put his mouth around the pigs' automatic waterer and took a swig. "Can't always eat pizza." He wiped his wet face with a sleeve.

"That's disgusting." Eli laughed. "Worse than swallowing swill or eating bees."

"Not when you're a thirsty hunter." Keller sighed. "I just might go bear hunting for the next few days. Climb a tree and wait till I see one."

"It's not the time for hunting bears. They're still denned up." Eli looked at Keller. "Besides, Pa says you got to be twelve to shoot anything legal."

"Who says I'm not twelve?" Keller patted the top of Eli's head like he was Tater. "Besides, I didn't say nothing about shooting. It's bow and arrow season."

Eli had a bow and arrow set, too—a junior one—but he couldn't go telling Keller that. He figured Keller had a real one for sure—adult-sized and powerful enough to kill a bear when it wasn't bear season.

"The males come out if there's a break in the cold." Keller picked a fingernail clean with the tip of his jackknife. "If not, there's always squirrels, possums and turkeys."

"You can kill them with a bow and arrow, too?"

"You can kill a turkey with a rock, if you need to. But I prefer bear meat. Tastes just like chicken, you know."

Eli didn't think so. He'd tried some when Pa bagged one a few years ago. It was sweet and greasy like ketchup you forgot to shake. But he didn't want to tell that to Keller either.

Keller nudged a panting pig with the tip of his boot.

"What'll happen to your hogs when you're away?"

"They could lose a little weight. Specially Black Raspberry."

The Sour Patch pig looked over at Keller and burped up some pepperoni pizza.

"Won't your ma and pa feed them?" Eli hadn't seen them around much.

Keller took a clump of gravel and threw it at the horse barn. The panting pig just stood there hyperventilating, watching the stones hit the barn door.

"What's wrong with this one?" Eli asked.

"Candy bloat. Haven't been selling as much as I'd like and the expiration date passed on some. Can't sell old candy, so I gave it to the hogs instead. He'll burp it out." Keller scratched the pig's prickly ears, then took a bucket and filled it with water.

"It's contagious, you know—scours." Keller brought the water bucket to the panting pig. "Don't get too close to that calf of yours or you'll get the runs, too."

Chapter Four

❧

Don't Let Go!

"Nobody's gonna be changing Little Joe," Grandpa said.

Eli poked his head under the bull calf to make sure. He smiled. Keller'd been wrong.

"He's the spittin' image of his sire, Apple Wood." Grandpa patted the top of Little Joe's shoulder. "And his grandsire, too. Sweet Cider made it all the way to the State Fair."

Eli liked finding Grandpa in the barn whenever he came home from school, even though he wasn't sure Pa did. But Pa never told stories like Grandpa. Or treated the barn like family. Eli knew how Grandpa's own pa had built the barn by hand, hauling bluestone for the foundation behind a stubborn ox with horns as wide as a tractor.

How the smell of the plank walls was like family and how you never washed your chore coat so the animals would smell that you were family, too.

Spider hopped into the hay manger. She dug deep and found Little Joe a mouse. It tried to wriggle free, but Spider kept it under her paw, waiting for Little Joe to notice. Little Joe sniffed at the mouse, then Spider chased it up the stanchion wall.

"Calmest thousand-pound bull you'd ever seen, Sweet Cider was," Grandpa said. "And so meaty and thick in the brisket, see." Grandpa poked at the dimpled spot below Little Joe's chest. The sudden move made the bull calf take a step back. "But when Sweet Cider walked into that show ring—seemed like he was floating, he was so light on his feet. Know how I know?" Grandpa took off his glasses and wiped them across his green Dickies coat. "'Cause I was there. Watchin' your pa all in his whites, fussin' with his milking cap in the dairy barn, waiting for his class. Got me so nervous I headed to the show ring and watched the beef show. I'd seen plenty of bulls at dairy shows—dairy bulls are downright nasty, I tell you. They could kill a man. But these beef bulls . . . calm as kittens."

Eli stretched down to stroke Spider and tried to imagine Pa in a milking cap, vanilla white and starchy. He wondered which cow Pa'd taken to the State Fair. "What number was that, Grandpa?" he asked. "The milker Pa took to the State Fair?"

Grandpa snorted at the cold wind. "It was Old Gertie's ma—Hattie." He picked off a piece of hay from the manger. "Just because you part with an animal or it might end up on your dinner plate don't mean you can't be nice to it . . . give 'em a name." Grandpa tossed the hay bit into the bedding. "That's where me and your pa disagree."

Little Joe sniffed Eli's hands for any treats, then butted Fancy's udder to get the milk to flow.

"Yes sir, nature sure is something." Grandpa bent down and eyed Little Joe. The calf's curly black lashes were shut tight while he suckled. "It knows Little Joe's drinking milk, not nibblin' on grass. And it sends that milk straight to the fourth stomach—no detours—so he gets the goods straightaway."

Eli knew cows had four stomachs, but he wasn't exactly sure why.

"Know how it knows?" Grandpa smiled. "'Cause Little Joe's sucking, not tearing up mouthfuls of grass. That's why if a calf don't nurse, you got to feed it through a baby bottle. Lapping up milk from a bucket won't get it to grow. Remember Old Gert and her last heifers? They were twins, and we fed Annabelle with a rubber lamb nipple, she was such a tiny thing."

Eli wondered where Annabelle was now.

Little Joe poked his head up, then licked his wet lips, making a smacking sound.

"Fancy's milk is all he needs right now. Once Little Joe starts grazing, nature'll see to it he chews the cud for hours, burping it up from the other stomachs till it's tender enough to be food."

Little Joe had nursed out. He gave Spider a sniff, then let her lick his milky muzzle.

The sun strengthened, and Eli could see the air move around Little Joe's moist whiskers. Dusty bits of grain floated past them and would soon settle over anything that didn't move, coating the barn with a powdery film.

"Nature sure made Little Joe a fine bull calf," Grandpa said. He pulled out a copy of the *Angus Journal* he'd rolled up in his back pocket. "Turn to page ten," he told Eli.

There was Apple Wood, standing in a field somewhere looking meaty and thick in the brisket, too. The advertisement said he had plenty of dimension and was more than just a numbers bull. That "his progeny exhibit flawless phenotype with show-winning appeal."

All Eli knew was that Apple Wood had a shiny gold ring through his nose and the calluses on his dewclaws were big as crab apples. Apple Wood's eyes were real tiny, too. Eli figured the bull could barely see through all that flesh and didn't know he had a nose ring, anyhow. The back of his black neck puffed out so thick, it was as if Tater, or a farm dog just like him, had climbed up and wrapped around Apple Wood's shoulders.

"Folks around here know all about his offspring." Grandpa swept his hand alongside Little Joe's back. "How most of them have just the right amount of marbling on their tops—and around the rib."

Little Joe yawned as Grandpa's fingers felt his rib cage. "We'll have buyers looking before Little Joe gets to the fair, I suspect."

Grandpa took the magazine and placed the picture of Apple Wood against Little Joe's girth. "Don't he look like him already, some?"

Little Joe licked the picture, then tried to grab the glossy ends with his tongue.

But Eli was focused on the folds in Little Joe's neck. Apple Wood didn't have folds; he had muscle. Little Joe didn't have any muscles to speak of and was no wider than Eli, except in the shoulders. His ears still looked silly, too, not cocked forward like Apple Wood's, but fuzzy as Hannah's slippers. And his switch wasn't even a real-looking switch yet. It hadn't reached anywhere near his hock.

"I mean, there's great possibility in that brisket, son, once you see past all that wrinkly flesh," Grandpa said.

Little Joe wandered over to the automatic waterer. A gush of water squirted into his eyes, so he pulled back his head, then stomped and mooed.

"See the skin?" Grandpa bent down and took hold of a fleshy fold. "He'll grow into it. That's why there's so much of it."

Little Joe flicked his ears and showed Grandpa the whites of his eyes. Then he shook his head and sneezed until Grandpa let go. "Course, growing gets pretty uncomfortable. And it itches. That's why he sneezes and scratches an awful lot."

Eli watched Little Joe take a pee and remembered how itchy his own ankles got last year, when he'd grown at least two inches.

"He's going through a red stage now, with his coat," Grandpa said. "Every Angus—at least the good ones— always go through one. But he's already square and walks easy. Look how long he is, too, how level his topline is. Just like Apple Wood."

Eli squinted and thought he could see how Little Joe might become just like Apple Wood. That Little Joe wouldn't always reach up to Eli's chest or follow him around the barn, his tiny hooves almost tickling whenever they stepped on Eli's muck boots, feeling more like plastic shoes. But then he stopped squinting and saw how squooshed Little Joe's muzzle still was. Eli felt the bull calf's hips and thought they were too bony to add volume to anything.

"Now don't look at his hips," Grandpa said. "Sure they're bony, but watch how wide he stands. He'll grow into them real soon."

Eli rubbed Little Joe's brisket while Grandpa put the *Angus Journal* back in his pocket.

"That's the sweet spot, Eli. Keep rubbin' on that and he'll forgive you for everything. Let you do most anything, too. Like getting him halter-broke."

Eli's heart pumped through his chore coat. "You mean right now?"

Grandpa nodded.

"But it's already getting dark." Eli looked down at the pen floor. He noticed their shadows moving against the sawdust and straw, the shifting light in the barn. He was pretty sure it must be close to five.

"Now's the best time to start, Eli. When he's kinda drowsy and full of milk and happy." Grandpa came out of the tack room with a rope halter to fit over Little Joe's muzzle, leaving enough length for Eli to use to lead.

Curious, Little Joe lowered his head, then came closer.

"Let 'im sniff it real good," Grandpa said.

Little Joe looked up at Eli and down to the halter.

"You should know right off the bat he's gonna fight it,"

Grandpa admitted. "It's just normal. Even though you've been befriending him. Now reach over and hand me that bucket of corn."

Eli wondered how he'd get the halter on Little Joe if there was a bucket of corn around.

"Put the halter in the bucket and when he reaches in to munch, slip it over his head." Grandpa's voice had turned faint and raspy.

Little Joe darted behind Fancy.

"Go ahead. Take him a little treat," Grandpa urged.

"You mean trick him," Eli said.

"Not exactly. You been with him every day, see. He trusts you. His first smell was you. You're the boss cow. Now go on. And don't make like you're doing something mean. He'll keep eating for a second or two, then start fightin' it. I'll grab the bucket once you got the halter on him."

Eli and Grandpa stood next to Fancy. She glanced at Eli and took a few steps back, rustling the straw bed as Little Joe hid deeper in the corner.

"Show him a handful of kernels," Grandpa whispered.

Slowly, Little Joe stepped out from the corner of the pen and over to Eli. He sniffed at the yellow niblets in Eli's palm and lowered his head into the bucket.

"That's it. Keep feeding him, lowering your hand until his face is deep inside. Now halter him."

As soon as Eli got the halter past Little Joe's eyes, the bull calf bucked back and thrashed his head from side to side. He swept the halter against his knees, trying to scrape it away, but Eli had already secured it.

"It's okay, boy," Eli murmured, holding the end of the halter snug. "I promise it won't hurt. Not if you don't keep rubbing."

Grandpa took the corn bucket and placed it under Fancy to keep her occupied. "Go on, Eli," Grandpa said. "Get up to him and scratch the back of his ears. Whatever you need to do to calm him."

Eli began to hum as he followed Little Joe around the pen. But Little Joe wouldn't let himself be soothed in any way and kept stutter-stepping about Fancy.

"Let him walk around with it for a little bit," Grandpa said. "See that it don't hurt."

Eli let go of the rope end and examined his palms. They'd gone all blotchy and swollen at the center, where the rope slivers had cut their way in.

Realizing he no longer had to fight, Little Joe lay down by Fancy and started chewing on the rope end.

"That halter's not a toy, Eli," Grandpa said. "Time to tie him up."

Grandpa helped Eli tie Little Joe's rope to the rail underneath the pen window. The bull calf bawled, getting

Fancy to come over. "Keep quïeting him," Grandpa prodded, rubbing Fancy's forehead.

"It's okay, boy." Eli spoke softly in Little Joe's ear. "How am I gonna take you to the fair if I can't even tie you to a post?"

Little Joe sniffed at the windowsill, then fought the rope. Over and over, Eli stroked the bull calf's chin. Finally, Little Joe gave it a rest.

"That's enough for today," Grandpa decided. "You don't want to sour him. And Fancy's been more than patient. Now take the halter off, give him some corn and keep rubbin' that brisket."

"Can we try again tomorrow, Grandpa?"

Grandpa squeezed Eli's shoulder. "Your pa will help you tomorrow. It's time for me to go home. Now get washed up for supper."

Eli waited until he couldn't see the taillights on Grandpa's Ford pickup anymore. Then he eyed Little Joe. He didn't want Pa helping him tomorrow, thinking he couldn't gentle his own bull calf. He had to show Little Joe who's boss. Or else Pa would. Eli'd lead him out to the silo and tie him up there for a few minutes, just to be sure. And he wouldn't let go. That's what Pa was always worried about.

Eli took the halter from his back pocket. He slid it up

on Little Joe's head so quickly Little Joe didn't see it coming. But when Eli led him out of the pen, the bull calf froze and started bawling.

"It's for the best, boy," Eli told him. "I need to make sure you know who's boss."

Eli kept tugging until he could hear Little Joe's hooves tapping on the barn's cement floor. *The silo's only a few more steps*, Eli thought. *I can see it through the barn window.*

Little Joe kept bawling and balking, pulling, then stopping, pulling, then stopping against the rope until frothy rings bubbled out of his mouth when they reached the silo.

"How else am I gonna lead you around?" Eli asked. "Get you into the show ring?"

Little Joe squinted and tugged harder on the rope.

Eli closed his eyes and tugged even harder than Little Joe. Then he felt a release. He wasn't tugging anymore. Little Joe was beside him, then bolting ahead of him at full gallop.

Don't let go was all Eli could think. His feet swept under him and he heard himself shout into his collar.

Eli could catch bits of the smoke-colored sky as Little Joe dragged him down the pasture hill. He felt a stab of pain whenever his chore coat rode up and the curly dock and chokeberry bushes beneath the snow jabbed at his skin.

Little Joe kept bawling and balking, pulling, then stopping, pulling, then stopping against the rope. . . .

"Help!" Eli yelled. He caught a burst of Hannah's pink coat and her cowboy boots running. He could hear Tater barking before something sharp tore through his sleeve, smothering the shouting. Mud coated Eli's eyes when Little Joe finally stopped. Eli blinked and forced one eye open.

They were at the bottom of the field, halfway through the fence, in front of the apple orchard. Little Joe was breathing hard. Eli could feel his arm moving up and down with the breath. He strained to lift his head and saw the bull calf's nostrils flaring. There were streaks of blood running down Eli's palm onto the rope, and his butt hurt. But he hadn't let go.

Tater caught up and came over, panting. He licked Eli's nose.

"Pa, come quick!" Hannah hollered. "Eli and Little Joe are covered in muck."

Chapter Five

❧

Mending Fences

Eli fought to keep still. Between Ma's scissors sending prickly bits of hair down his back and the stitches he got in his hand the night before, Eli was one big itch. The Easter lily sitting at the center of the kitchen table wasn't helping. The scent from its curled-out petals kept prickling Eli's nose.

"Ma, can you move that flower?" Eli wished he could get to his nose, but he was pinned underneath the hair-cutting cape.

"What for?" Ma asked. She stopped clipping for a second.

"'Cause it stinks." Eli caught another whiff. He thought

about the forgotten cantaloupes going rotten in Grandpa's garden last summer.

"It's part of Easter, Eli," Ma said. She stuck a finger in the planter, making the purple tinfoil crinkle.

"Just like Easter bunnies." Hannah grinned. She combed the white fur rounding Sleepy's back while the bunny nibbled on a carrot top.

"Hold still," Ma told Eli. Her eyes darted from Eli's bangs to the scissors.

"Colored eggs are part of Easter, too," Hannah said. "Ma, you promised we'd color eggs tonight and now you're cutting Eli's hair."

"Well, I didn't know about the honor roll pictures until tonight. There'll be plenty of time to color eggs tomorrow. Eli has to get a haircut."

"No, I don't." Eli squeezed his eyes shut as Ma squirted water on his bangs.

"Yes, you do." Ma gripped Eli's shoulders. "I can't have you looking shaggy in the picture. The whole town knows I cut hair."

"Not the shoulders, Ma!" Eli flinched. "They're sore, too."

"You don't get it halter-broke the first time." Pa's voice came out of nowhere.

Eli bolted upright, nearly catching Ma's scissors and

another cut. He'd barely noticed Pa reading *Lancaster Farming* by the pellet stove.

"The animal's just not that smart," Pa added.

"Little Joe's plenty smart," Hannah shouted. "How would *you* like a rope around your head?"

"Hush, Hannah," Ma whispered. "Don't be smarting off to your pa."

"Well, it's true." Hannah kissed Sleepy's ears.

For once Eli agreed with Hannah. He wouldn't want that rope halter around his face. He knew how it felt just holding it with his hand—tore off a chunk of skin nearly an inch deep.

"We ain't cows." Pa stretched the words out slowly. "Born better than that."

Pa spit out the last part strong as a fist.

"Little Joe was just actin' out," Eli said softly. "It wasn't his fault."

"Treat them all neighborly and you're asking for trouble." Pa clenched his paper and exhaled. "Next thing you know, we'll be having a picnic in the pastures with them cows. And living off potato salad instead of beef."

"I could live off potato salad," Hannah said.

"Put the beef industry out of business," Pa complained.

"Chet, did you notice the price of eggs in the

supermarket lately?" Ma asked. "The fancy ones?" Ma was good at turning the subject over.

Pa grumbled, refusing to look up from the paper. All Eli caught was Pa's hand reaching for his cup of coffee.

"They call them free-range," Ma said, tilting Eli's head with a finger. "Which just means their chickens wander the fields like ours do."

Pa turned the page and buried his face deeper into *Lancaster Farming*.

"They get nearly two dollars more a dozen. It's something to think about, Chet. We used to have a sign out on the lawn saying BROWN EGGS FOR—"

"We. Don't. Sell. Eggs." Pa made a rustling noise with the newspaper before he let go. He went over to the coffee-maker and poured himself another cup of black coffee.

"Tess is coming over," Hannah announced.

Eli's chest froze.

"To teach me how to mane-braid like they do at the horse shows."

"Did you hear that, Chet?" Ma took the neck brush to Eli's ears, tickling the stray hairs away. "I bet Tess'll bring you some real milk."

Tess'll be getting her honor roll picture taken, too, Eli thought. *In the fifth-grade class.*

Sometimes Eli got off the school bus with Tess, saying he'd rather walk the rest of the mile home. Then he'd lie on his back in the meadow nearby, knee-deep in clover. Eli waited for the thundering of hooves and Tess nickering to get her Appaloosa to jump. He'd only look up when he heard a pause in the ring below—right when they'd both caught the wind—and horse and rider leapt into the air, clearing the rails.

"Ma, can you hurry up?" Eli said, fidgeting. There was no way he was going to be caught getting his hair cut in front of Tess.

"Just a few more wisps in the back, Eli," Ma promised. "I'll be careful going around the scratches." The cold sides of the scissors skimmed his neck.

"Maybe Tess'll buy one of my Easter bunnies. I've only got two dwarfs left." Hannah put Sleepy in the rabbit crate. "And Snow White's gonna kindle again in a month, so I'll have eight more."

"She's got enough animals of her own to take care of," Eli said. He tried to sound funny, like he didn't care if Tess came over or not, but it came out kind of mean.

"They've only got one house pet—Blue." Hannah sounded hurt. "And he's getting really old."

Pa lifted the top of the coffeemaker and poured his cup back into the filter. He never got used to store-bought milk. Said it tasted all runny and that the color wasn't natural. Like they bleached it white or something. Eli could barely remember what real milk tasted like, but he knew they could drink as much as they wanted. That it was more cream and had a grassy smell to it—like clover and alfalfa chopped up. Pa drank it warm without shaking. He didn't care about mixing the top part and the bottom part together.

"There." Ma gave Eli a smile. "All finished."

Eli tugged at the shiny cape with all the daisies on it. He hoped to wrench it free but banged his sore hand instead. "Ouch!" Eli shook his stitched-up palm and tried not to show how much it stung.

"I'll get the ointment," Ma said.

"Does it hurt a lot, Eli?" Hannah asked. "Here. Take Happy." She scooped up another bunny between her arms and placed the white clump on Eli's lap. "Give his fur a few strokes and you'll feel better." She smiled. "Mini-lops are the most lovable buns in the world."

Eli felt Happy's whiskers moving while the bunny sniffed. He clung to Eli's thighs with his nails and blinked his ruby-colored eyes. Eli touched the droopy ears to get the bunny to stop shaking and could see the pink skin right through the fur.

"Should I take the bandage off?" Ma asked. "And rub some more cream in?"

Eli shook his head.

Hannah put a bandage on the ruddy patch of moleskin

covering Eli's stitches. "This is from my Princess collection," she said. "It's my last Snow White."

It had black-haired princesses all over it. "Ah, why'd you go and do that, Hannah?" Eli moaned.

The doorbell rang and there was Eli, in a haircutting cape covered with daisies, petting a bunny on his lap with a Snow White bandage on his bandage. He tore them all off and got Happy to hop onto the kitchen floor.

"Hey." Tess walked into the kitchen with a jug of fresh milk and a whole bunch of yarn.

"Hey." Eli fingered the tablecloth and saw that his stitches were oozing blood.

"Nice to see you, Tess." Ma took Tess's coat and put it on a kitchen chair. "Oh, how thoughtful. Did you see, Chet? Tess brought us some milk."

Ma took the jug and put it in the fridge. "How 'bout I bake a batch of chocolate chip cookies to go with that milk?"

"Yum!" Hannah squealed. She nudged Happy into the rabbit crate with Sleepy. "Can you make 'em extra gooey? And have Eli promise he won't eat more than his share?"

Eli blushed. He was glad Tess could barely see him, with the Easter lily and all. He didn't know what to do with his hands anymore, so he leaned over, stuck a finger in the planter like Ma did and got a chin full of dusty bits from the creamy petals.

"Hear you got stitches." Tess rested against the kitchen table and looked down at Eli's hand.

"It's nothin'."

"His bull calf did it," Hannah blurted.

"Little Joe?" Tess asked.

"Uh-huh." Hannah smiled and put her unicorn-mane-braiding kit on the kitchen table. "He's the reason Eli got torn up. He dragged Eli all the way down the hill to the apple orchard and Eli never let go."

Tess put the balls of pink yarn on the kitchen counter. "I got my foot caught in a stirrup once. Yanked it pretty bad at my biggest show. I didn't do well, but I'm glad me and Chili Pepper ended up okay."

That's how Eli felt. Eli was glad Little Joe turned out to be okay. He didn't care about the stitches.

"Good thing you brought real milk," Hannah said, brushing her unicorn's mane. "Pa spits out store-bought milk every time. It makes Ma so mad. First, he makes a funny face right before he does it, then he marches over to the sink and just spits it out."

"We can hear you, Hannah," Ma reminded her, scooping out flour from the pantry. "Tess, has your mother's perm relaxed by now?" Ma asked.

"It's perfect, Mrs. Stegner." Tess smiled. "More like the ripples from a French braid than a poodle's fur."

Hannah looked up at Tess. "Can you show me how to mane-braid?" she asked. "I already know how to braid regular. Ma taught me."

Tess leaned over, took Hannah's fingers and reached for the unicorn's purple mane. "Let's do rosebud braids," she said. "First you divide a handful of hair into three strands, like this."

Eli pretended not to listen. He pulled up a chair next to Pa, taking a section of *Lancaster Farming*.

"After you're finished braiding, you take the yarn—" Tess glanced over at the kitchen counter, where she'd left the bright pink balls of yarn.

Eli had them in his hands before Tess could move.

"Thanks." Tess smiled. "You take a piece of yarn and thread it into the needle. That's good, Hannah. And sew it through the braid, up to the crest. Who did the stitches?"

Was Tess talking to him?

"The Krakowski girl," Ma said, mixing the dough. "She's working in the emergency room now."

"I thought so. Hannah, look at this technique." Tess pointed to Eli's hand. "It's hunter style. She shows jumpers. She did a really nice job of it."

"If Little Joe goes lame, you could win a blue ribbon

with your stitches, Eli." Hannah tilted her chair back and laughed.

"He ain't lame." Eli put his sore hand in his pocket. "He'll take the blue ribbon."

Pa sat up straighter, folded his section of the newspaper and half smiled at Eli. "Let's go outside and finish mending that fence your bull calf tore through," he said.

"Chet, shouldn't he wait until the stitches heal?"

"I'm fine, Ma."

Ma came over and spread a bandage across Eli's palm, careful not to make it too tight.

"Come on, Tater," Eli called. He was out the door before he remembered he didn't say goodbye to Tess.

"Cookies will be ready in half an hour!" Ma hollered from the porch. "Make sure you put on gloves, Eli. It's still winter. Even if it is the tail end of March." Ma threw on the porch lights and lingered at the door. "Careful not to brush against my lilac shoots."

But Eli could tell that the deer had already nibbled the first buds clean off the branches.

It had been dark for a while and cloudy. Tater jumped through the murky air into the truck bed and waited for Eli to catch up. Eli slid against the back of the cab and tapped at the window to let Pa know they were ready. He hung on to Tater as the Silverado zigzagged down the pasture and watched Ma's silhouette in the doorway's amber glow get smaller.

Eli and Pa worked together in silence, fixing the fence he'd rammed into with Little Joe. Burrowing his boots into the muddy trail the pickup's tires had made, Eli uncoiled the spool of barbed wire. Pa wrapped it around the fence post, drawing it snug before cutting it with pliers.

The only noise Eli could hear was the motor of the Silverado running. And sometimes Tater. He barked whenever a white-tailed deer darted across the pasture.

The last of the barbed wire found a weak spot in Eli's glove. He flinched as it bit into his sore hand. Eli stopped feeding the wire to Pa and pulled off his glove.

"Still bleedin'?" Pa asked.

Eli nodded and stroked the bandage to keep it from curling up. He shivered inside his jacket and put the glove back on. Digging his boots into the wheel marks once more, Eli tried to find traction, but the ridges of mud had frozen up.

"It'll callus up soon," Pa said. "Rope burns always do. First they crack open, then they heal and harden up for good."

Eli followed the yellow high beams lighting up the fence posts. He tried to catch sight of Pa's eyes, but they were blocked by the brim of Pa's Chevy cap.

Had Pa hardened up for good?

Eli reached for the spool, not quite knowing what to say. "Little Joe came out of it okay," he mumbled.

Pa tugged at the top wire to see if it felt secure. "First thing in the morning, Eli, you get back in the barn and show that calf who's boss."

Eli focused on the frosty billows of Pa's breath as Pa picked up a rotted oak branch and threw it for Tater to fetch.

"Have Ma wrap some gauze over your hand and you won't feel a thing."

Eli watched the glints of silver wire coiling out from between his gloves, wondering why Pa hated cows so much. He'd been around them all his life, same as Eli, only they didn't seem to make Pa happy. Eli always felt better knowing there were cattle around. He'd look out the window and there the cows were, chomping or sniffing. Coming off the school bus, he'd catch a glimpse of them huddled up beside the pines and out of the wind, blinking at him. Or he'd spot the tops of their backs, knowing that when he got closer, their chunky necks would be outstretched, skimming the grasses for food.

Eli looked up and saw Ma in the stream of the pickup's high beams, clutching her coat to her ribs. "Ned Kinderhoff called," she said.

Pa's jaw tightened, but he kept twisting the wire around the post.

"He wants you at the sawmill by six in the morning."

Pa jabbed the rim of his cap with his thumb. "He knows I won't say no," Pa mumbled.

Ma came over and stood by Pa. "We need the money, Chet." Ma lowered her voice, but Eli still heard. He knew all about Ned Kinderhoff. He grew pumpkins bigger than Pa's and beat him out at the fair. Whenever they sat down to dinner without Pa, it was because of Ned Kinderhoff.

"We're all done here, Eli," Pa said.

Tater barked at Hannah running down the pasture, her mittens hanging from her neck. "Can I ride in the back of the truck with Tater and Eli, too, Pa?" Hannah asked.

Pa nodded.

"Come on, Tater." Eli knew they were both in for a ride full of talking.

"Can I mane-braid Little Joe's tail, Eli? Now that I know how?"

"No."

"How come? He's your show animal."

"'Cause it's not right. He's a boy."

"Then I'll mane-braid Fancy's tail."

"No."

"Why not?"

"'Cause she needs it to take care of Little Joe and swish flies away. Go find yourself a unicorn."

Hannah went silent for a moment and looked up at the

night sky. Tater crouched down low and dug his head under Hannah's mitten, looking for a belly rub or even just a scratch.

"You have to believe in unicorns before they'll show." Hannah turned to face Eli. "And the *whole* family's got to believe."

Eli wasn't sure what he believed. He looked down at his glove and wondered if his sore hand would be ready by tomorrow. And if he really wanted it to be. He'd promised that nothing would happen to Little Joe. Now he'd gone and made the bull calf afraid and sent him fleeing clear across the pasture.

"Unicorns can't be tamed, either." Hannah scratched the knuckle on Tater's head. "Not like Tater. Or Little Joe."

Eli wasn't really sure if Little Joe could be tamed.

"Unless—" Hannah stuck the word right out in the air.

"Unless what?" Eli asked.

"Unless they're absolutely certain nobody'll hurt them."

Chapter Six

Sorry

Eli brought two halters into the barn, some apples and a brush. He didn't know what to expect. He'd gone back this morning like Pa'd told him to, but Little Joe seemed tinier than Eli'd remembered. He still fit under Fancy and was bunched up like a blanket between her legs. So mostly, Eli just stared at the two standing close together and let them be.

When Eli got home from school, Little Joe was curled up in the straw, his legs all folded together as he slept. When he heard Eli, Little Joe shook his ears and yawned. He lunged forward to get to his knees, uncurling his back legs first, then the front, till he was standing.

"It's gonna be different today, boy," Eli whispered.

Little Joe eyed the two rope halters laced through Eli's arms. Eli brought them over to let him sniff, but the calf skittered behind Fancy.

"Sorry 'bout the last time." Eli slid one halter carefully across his bandaged hand. "It was all my fault. I tried to hurry you." Eli walked with the halter over to Fancy. She closed her eyes and stuck out her neck as Eli put it around her head. Then he tied the end to the rail under the window. "See?" Eli peeked around Fancy to get a look at Little Joe. "It's nothing to get bothered about. Really."

Eli pulled out a currycomb from his back pocket, reached up and started brushing Fancy all over. She stood still, taking in the feeling, her switch raising a bit as Eli got near the back. Then Eli started to hum. "Every cow likes to be brushed," he said. "But they got to be tied up first."

Eli felt a warm breath on his brushing hand. Then a wet mouth. "Wanna sniff?" he asked. Little Joe had come over. Eli showed him the brush. Little Joe breathed in the bristles, then play-nibbled at the handle.

"From now on, no more secrets," Eli promised. "Or being sneaky. You'll see what you're getting into."

Little Joe took a step closer, eyed the halter on Eli's arm and sniffed it. Then he went over and sniffed Fancy's.

"It's the same thing, boy." Eli showed Little Joe his halter. "Should we give it another try?" Eli slid the halter slowly over Little Joe's head. This time, Little Joe didn't fight when Eli tied him to the rail next to Fancy.

Spider leapt onto the windowsill, her paws stained flaxen from months of barn prowling. She shook the furry necklace of stripes on her chest and looked down at Little Joe.

"Keeping an eye on your calf, huh, Spider?" Eli pulled out another comb from his pocket, then started brushing Little Joe, too. His bandaged hand stung at first as he stood between the two cows, brushing. He'd stroke one, then the other, like he was swimming the front crawl lopsided; Little Joe chest-high to him, Fancy taller than Eli. "Wanna know something?" Eli asked them.

Little Joe's ears pricked up. He let himself be swayed by the movement as Eli brushed his neck. "You get brushed a lot at the fair," Eli said. "I'll brush you at least ten times a day. And you'll get the blower on you, too."

Fancy turned around and glanced at Eli.

"I can try it on you, too, Fancy. First time you get a bath this spring." Eli was down near both rumps now, about ready to brush their tails. "Pa says Ned Kinderhoff grows pumpkins two rumps wide. He don't know how, but he'd like to find out. They're so heavy the judge at the fair's got to use a forklift to weigh them."

Spider's back arched and she extended her black claws as a draft came through the window, blowing in the last bits of winter. Little Joe peered under Spider's legs and out the window. "Keller says there's a Ferris wheel right near the show barn. If we get a row on that side, you can see it. Or if you want a quiet one, Pa says we just get there early and park a chair where we want to be."

Little Joe's eyes began to close as Eli got to the switch.

"And when you win the blue ribbon, they announce it over the loudspeaker." Eli came up to Little Joe's head. "They got bleachers high as corn silos and they're loaded with people looking down at you."

Little Joe brought his muzzle close to Eli's chore coat and smelled the apple in Eli's pocket. "You wanna try an apple?" Eli took out a slice and reached over to give one to Fancy first, but Little Joe snatched it instead. "There'll be plenty of good stuff to chew when you go on pasture next month." Little Joe nudged at Eli's pocket for more slices. "After weaning. First clover. Then apples, come summer. Sure seems like you're ready. And you won't have to drag me down the field to get to it." Eli laughed and looked out the window. It had started to rain.

There were still patches of snow, lumped on the lawn like dirty snow cones. But it wasn't snowing; it was raining.

Eli got closer to Fancy and gave the last apple slice to her. "Pretty soon it's gonna be Big Night," Eli whispered, his pulse quickening. He'd never seen one before but knew what it meant. "That's when little, tiny creatures no longer than your ears come out of hiding." Eli scratched one of Fancy's ears. "In the middle of the night. It'll get warmer after that," Eli assured them. "Then you'll be in the pastures in no time chewing on apples."

Chapter Seven

Big Night

Grandpa was peering out from his kitchen window when Pa dropped Eli off for dinner like he did every Wednesday night. And there was one more tractor seat in Grandpa's collection, mounted on the red barn.

"Pick what you want for dessert, Eli." Grandpa smiled. He was peeling a potato and came into the sun porch wearing one of Grandma's aprons up high around his chest.

Eli could smell something good cooking as he passed rows of lumpy old hats and Pa's blue ribbons pinned on the beams.

"Go on now." Grandpa tapped his peeling knife against the freezer lid. "I'll lift it open and you reach. Everything's labeled."

It was the kind of freezer you stuck your head in, then leaned over, careful not to tip onto the bags of frozen peaches. There were jars of gooseberry jam underneath and those thumbprint cookies Hannah liked.

Eli dug deeper and spotted licorice stripes. They came from an orange tub of homemade Tiger Tiger ice cream. Below it was a layer of square pizza Grandpa learned to make when he was in the army and lived in Italy.

"Don't matter what you pick or how you mix it," Grandpa said, poking his head through cloudy pockets of freezer air. "Tiger Tiger with pizza can be nice. So can gooseberry jam over peaches."

Eli chose Tiger Tiger ice cream, then square pizza for later.

"Salisbury steak's for supper, Eli. Know what's in the secret sauce?"

Eli smiled. "Something with tomatoes."

Grandpa loved growing tomatoes. Said it gave him something to fuss over, with Grandma gone and no milkers to take care of anymore.

"We'll make 'em into sandwiches tonight," Grandpa said. He pointed to a loaf of bread puffed out beyond the pan. "Turn it over. It should come out if you tap the bottom."

Eli tapped twice and the loaf came out.

"You can cut 'er up, then get out the wax paper."

Grandpa lowered the stove burner and the pan stopped sizzling. "We'll be having those Salisbury steak sandwiches—to go."

Eli's heart skipped a beat. He knew it was raining out and that it was April, but it seemed kind of early. Winter had just ended.

"Tonight could be Big Night, Eli. I can feel it."

Eli stopped cutting.

"Ever have Salisbury steak by a pond with thousands of spotted salamanders and spring peepers to keep you company? How 'bout it?"

Eli cut the bread slices as thick as his wrist to get to the end of the loaf. "Do you think they're out right now?" He couldn't wait to see salamanders and peeper frogs.

"Let's see." Grandpa spooned his special sauce onto the steaks and looked at Eli. "Suppose we'll have to check the thermometer outside to make sure."

Eli ran to the thermometer hanging on the back porch and stuck his head out. He followed the red line with his finger. "It says forty-three degrees, Grandpa."

"That's about right," Grandpa said, making the wax paper crackle as he folded it around the sandwiches. "Can you just imagine, Eli, living underground most of your life? Then one day, something inside you tells you to get out from that hole and crawl a quarter mile to a pond?"

Grandpa stuffed the sandwiches into a bucket. "You don't mind Salisbury steak sandwiches with triple sauce on 'em, do you? It's got green pepper in it, you know. Not just tomatoes."

"What's wrong with green peppers?" Eli pulled on his boots before straightening his socks and got out the hat from his slicker.

"Your pa always hated Salisbury steak," Grandpa said. "Don't know why. Specially if it had green peppers in it." He reached for the straw hat on the hook next to Grandma's apron and stuck it on his head before heading out the door.

"That's just about the silliest hat I've ever seen, Grandpa." Eli laughed.

"Scare the trucks away." Grandpa winked. "Or at least, get 'em to slow down some. Not too many folks around here wearing bright yellow straw hats on a rainy night. Now which bucket you want?" He lifted the handle in his left hand, then the right. "One's for eatin' and one's for leadin' critters."

Eli eyeballed them both. "I'll take the leading one," he said, peering into the empty bucket he just took.

"That's good, Eli. Always look down." Grandpa nodded. "Remember, animals come first tonight. It's their night. And you never know what's at your feet." Grandpa took out the gleaming silver flashlight from his slicker and aimed it into the night. "Could be the biggest spotted salamander of 'em all."

Eli tiptoed over the lawn past the apple orchard like he was walking on eggshells. He lifted the heels of his Billy boots every so often to see if he'd squashed anything.

A thick veil of fog covered the valley in a tarp of chalky white, weaving threads of mist around Grandpa and Eli. It carried with it the smell of green—the newness coming to life in the brush nearby.

Lemony green ferns splayed out below, their leaves in tight fists, refusing to break through the hairy skin until it warmed up.

Eli was surprised how cold forty-something degrees was. The cool mist uncurled in swirling bits, dipping in and out of the sky ahead of them. He strained to hear a spring peeper or even a bullfrog, but the night was quiet. Just the rhythm of the rain tapping lightly on their shoulders, following them as they reached pavement.

It was a steady rain, the kind of wetness that comes from all over, like the sprayers you walked through to keep cool at the fair. It got into places regular rain didn't. Eli could already feel it seeping down the back of his neck in the gap between his hat and the slicker. His face was moist and clammy, too, but it didn't bother him. He knew something was about to happen. Something hardly anyone got to see.

"They'll be crossing the road over the top of the hill if they cross at all," Grandpa called out.

Eli'd gotten ahead of Grandpa, stretching his footsteps farther and farther as he aimed for the crossing. He'd seen the spot during the day—Grandpa pointed it out plenty of times—but he'd never been to a crossing. *Too young to stay up half the night*, Pa used to say. *And get soaked right through*, Ma would add.

Not tonight.

Eli hesitated when he heard the sound of wet tires skimming over the slick pavement behind them. Was it coming toward them? He turned to look at Grandpa.

"Uh-oh." Grandpa shook his head. "Stay on the side of the road, Eli. He might be turning."

But the car whooshed straight instead.

"I see something!" Eli ran up to the yellow lines on the pavement covering the hill.

"Careful, Eli." Grandpa beamed the flashlight on it.

"It's a big one, Grandpa!"

"That's a spotted salamander, Eli."

Eli watched its slimy orange body creep over the yellow lines. The salamander's long, spotted tail swished behind four tiny legs. Eli wondered how those legs got it this far. He knelt on the other side in the gravel to catch it.

"Just like in a dinosaur movie, ain't it?" Grandpa smiled.

Eli watched its slimy orange body creep over the yellow lines.

"He's longer than my hand, Grandpa. And there's another one right behind it."

"Those'd be the males. They come first. The females follow."

"There's another one, wiggling through the grass. They keep coming, Grandpa!"

"Let's help them along, Eli. Fill the bucket."

Eli loaded his bucket with salamanders, trying not to squeeze too hard but holding them long enough to feel their rubbery bodies. *Just like Tater's chew toys*, Eli thought as they squirmed along the pink ridges where his stitches had been. *But slipperier and wet.* Eli dumped the bucket of salamanders on the other side of the road. He listened to the rustling of grass as they slithered through, scurrying to get to the pond.

A brightness far stronger than Grandpa's flashlight struck the side of Eli's face as he knelt, blinding him for a moment. A motor rose higher than the hum of the rain as the swish of tires came closer.

"Can't we make 'em stop?" Eli asked.

"And get us all killed? Get up, Eli." Grandpa clutched Eli's chest against his. "We can only hurry so many of them along."

Grandpa and Eli stood on the side of the road, holding their buckets while the high beams came toward them, then past. As soon as they'd gone, Eli rushed onto the road again to scoop up more salamanders. He went to lift one up and noticed another splayed on the pavement, its tail flattened and lifeless. Eli put it in the bucket anyway, just in case he was wrong and it had a chance.

"How come they cross the road, Grandpa? Can't they go another way?"

"You mean a safer way?" Grandpa clutched two salamanders. "Been crossing this way for hundreds of years, Eli. Maybe thousands. It's what they were born to do."

The salamanders squirted out of Grandpa's hands and onto safety in the grass. "They follow the path their ancestors took," Grandpa said. "And no road's gonna stop 'em. They cross it. If they go, they go. And that's the end of it. Good night. You can't beat a truck. But you know what, son? Enough of them do. Then they head to the pond and find themselves a mate."

Before Eli and Grandpa got to the pond, Eli could already hear the high-pitched shrill of peeper frogs.

"They're calling for a mate, Eli. That's what brings 'em to the pond."

Once they'd made it to the clearing, Grandpa shone his flashlight over the water. "Go on now, get closer, Eli."

Eli gazed into the pond and caught his breath. Salamanders covered the water, swimming forward and backward and in circles. Some looked like they were hugging, others chasing each other in a game of hide-and-seek. Two salamanders looped around. Eli caught a glimpse of their wrinkly white bellies before they broke the surface with their spotted faces, then swam away.

"Look at the branches, Eli." Grandpa pointed to some sticks jutting out of the pool.

Eli stared at the see-through blobs slick as marbles building on the branches. Right before his eyes they grew thicker—like cotton candy—as if spun by invisible hands. Swirling thicker and thicker, the egg clusters sparkled until the brown of the branches could barely be seen.

"Those'll be tadpoles in a few months. Or sallies. I can't tell from here," Grandpa said, squinting. "There's hundreds of 'em."

Plop plop, just like kernels popping, Eli heard frogs leap into the water, while others called for a mate. The screeching sound pierced right through him. On any other day, Eli would've pressed his palms against his ears to drown out the noise. But tonight it sounded perfect. It didn't seem too loud at all.

"Funny, ain't it?" Grandpa sat on a moss-lined stump and smiled. "How you don't hear a lick of a frog for five months. Then all of a sudden, one night, there they are, peeping like they've always been there." Grandpa pointed at a peeper clinging to a log. "Tryin' to impress the females." He rolled his eyes as the peeper's throat puffed out to bursting. "From now on, Eli, you can keep your bedroom window open. You'll hear them calling."

"How do you know, Grandpa?"

"'Cause it used to be my window. I remember the house was so still at night, you couldn't hear one breath. So I listened for their peeps. That's how I knew the rest of the world was still out there." Grandpa reached for the eating bucket. "How 'bout toasting the night with a sandwich?" He handed Eli the biggest one. "Grandma liked coming here, too," Grandpa said. "She called it one of nature's little miracles."

They both watched a salamander crawl over Eli's boot to get to the water.

"*Put them in the bucket and keep the rhythm of life going*, she'd say. They got the same right to be here as we do. We just happen to be in charge most days." Grandpa wiped off the Salisbury steak sauce on Eli's cheek with a finger. "At least we think we are. Times like this, when they remind us Mother Nature's in charge."

Eli smiled and watched a salamander swirl up to circle another, then back down again to the murky bottom of the pond. "It's like they're spinning eggs," Eli said. "Magical eggs clear as glass." Everywhere he looked, there were branches coated with eggs. "And there's so many of them, it just don't seem real."

"Sometimes we ain't used to real," Grandpa said. "So when we see it, we don't even recognize it."

"They don't notice we're here, do they?" Eli smiled as a peeper hopped onto his coat and dove into the pond.

"Naw. They're so bent on finding a mate, for one night, we don't even exist."

"Don't they get tired?" Eli asked.

"Will you be tired when you win the blue ribbon?"

Eli knew he wouldn't be.

"You wouldn't even feel how heavy the hay bale was at the end of the day, would you?"

Eli smiled and shook his head.

"I expect they'll go on even longer," Grandpa said. "Maybe for a few more nights yet."

"Then what happens?" Eli watched a salamander slip into the water.

"The big ones go back to their homes under the leaves, and the eggs hatch in a couple weeks without 'em." Grandpa put the wax paper back in the bucket. "From now on the valley won't be silent. Until we forget again and one morning in the fall, we wake up late thinking, *What's wrong? Why's it so quiet?* And remember the peepers have buried themselves in the ground and gone to sleep half froze." Grandpa turned to Eli. "You must be cold."

Eli's teeth were chattering, but he didn't want to leave.

"Time for us to go back, too, Eli."

When they reached the road, a set of headlights came toward them. It was Pa's pickup.

Eli stepped into the road and waved his hands to flag down Pa. "You can't go no further, Pa. The salamanders need to cross." Eli looked at the pavement. "You already squashed two."

"Oh, fer cryin' out loud." Pa stuck his head out of the truck.

"I would've dropped him off, Chet." Grandpa cupped his hands to cut out the glare from the high beams. "Is it time already?"

"It's nearly ten." Pa's jaw was tight as he stared down Grandpa. "When was the last time a boy his age stayed up this late?"

"When you were nine, Chet." Grandpa lifted up his bucket. "It's salamander night. Don't you remember?"

"It's a school night. Get in the truck, Eli."

Eli looked at Pa, then up at Grandpa.

"Go on, son," Grandpa said.

Eli handed him the bucket.

"Careful backing up, Chet." Grandpa spoke louder than Eli'd been used to. "Those Silverados haven't been the same since that recall."

Eli hopped in the truck and Pa backed up. The rain

sounded tinny bouncing off the hood. Beyond it, Eli tried to focus on Grandpa, but Pa'd switched the wipers to high. Eli could only see him in flashes, dipping in and out of the windshield.

Pa U-turned it home and Eli swung near him. Through the rearview mirror he saw Grandpa just standing there, holding both buckets and grinning.

Chapter Eight

❧

Missing Mama

All kinds of birds Eli'd forgotten about warbled and cooed outside the barn. They made nests in the river maples that were so thick with buds, it was as if winter never happened. A cluster of downy chicks snuck out of the barn chasing cottony strands of willow dander. Even drowsy flies buzzed to life, pesking around Little Joe's ears. He stood tied up beside Fancy, filled out and high as her chin and past Eli's shoulders.

It was still early. The peepers made noise in the swollen creek nearby. Eli knew they must be the little eggs he'd seen with Grandpa all hatched and swimming in the water.

"Their mamas lay eggs just like jelly beans," Eli said, feeding Little Joe an apple slice. "And they don't take long to hatch. Not nine months like you, Fancy. It only takes a couple weeks." Eli gave her a slice, too.

"Everything in nature's being born around here!" Grandpa's eyes lit up as he entered the barn. "Peepers, chicks, flies." He swatted at one, then looked at Fancy and Little Joe. "But it don't come without heartache."

Eli wondered whose heart Grandpa was talking about. Probably Little Joe's and Fancy's, since it was time for Little Joe to be weaned and put on pasture grass instead of milk.

Shades of green had taken over the brown patches dotting the fields. Clumps of young clover grew green as snap peas above the hill between the alfalfa. And pale olive rods of timothy stood nearly a foot high below, their tips blushing pink like ripened peaches.

"Out in Wyoming they let nature take care of the separation," Grandpa explained. "The ma drops another calf and her other baby—a yearling, oh, about seven months older than Little Joe—gets nudged away. Not with your pa."

"Don't have time to wait a year in this business," Pa said. He came into the barn carrying a lead strap with chains bigger than Eli'd seen before. "Costs too much. Need to get him on pasture and feed so he'll fatten out for the fair."

"Did you see, Pa?" Eli said. "I got them both haltered and tied up and they're not making a peep."

"Sure looks like he's ready to be weaned." Pa smiled. "Good thing you got him used to them apples. He won't miss the milk one bit."

"Need any help weaning, Chet?" Grandpa asked. "First-time mothers'll do anything to get to their calf."

"We'll be fine." Pa put the lead strap on a bale of hay. "Me and Eli can take care of things."

"Are we weaning today, Pa?" Eli asked.

"Right after I check the fence lines to see if they'll hold."

Grandpa came into the pen and stroked Fancy. "Make sure she gets bred soon, Chet. She's gonna need another baby to fuss over."

"Is Fancy gonna have another calf, Pa?" Eli asked.

"Maybe." Pa took out the pliers from his coat pocket. "Be ready to take 'em out when I get back, Eli."

Grandpa looked down at Little Joe. He eyed the bull calf in such a sad way, Eli got worried.

"Little Joe's gonna need all the attention he can get, Eli," Grandpa said. "Once he gets taken from Fancy, he'll bawl something awful. Probably the whole night through. And then some."

"Milkers don't do that." Eli rubbed at a patch where Little Joe's winter coat was still shedding. He'd seen milkers get weaned before. Even a heifer taken from its mother a day after birth. She got the bottle right away. She didn't seem to mind.

"Beef calves are the longest of all cattle to stay with their mothers," Grandpa said. "Still, it's like leavin' home when you're barely a teenager." Grandpa fiddled with the tuft of hair that stuck straight up on Little Joe's poll. "It's not the milk he needs; it's the company. He doesn't know he's ready yet. To be on his own."

This time Grandpa rubbed the top of Eli's head. "Let 'em sniff each other real good, Eli. I'll be down by Fancy's pasture to see she don't get cut up. No telling how desperate a mother will be when she can't find her calf. They're bent on taking care of that first baby forever."

Eli took off Little Joe's halter. He rubbed the sides of Little Joe's face where the rope left its mark, expecting the bull calf to flinch. Instead, Little Joe just stood there.

"Go on." Eli shoved Little Joe's rump closer to Fancy. But the calf thought Eli was playing and nibbled at his sleeve. "Get some milk!" Eli'd said it too loudly. Little Joe's head jerked up from the sudden sound.

"You don't know what today is," Eli whispered. "And I'm glad." He nudged the bull calf, softly this time, toward Fancy's black udder. Watching him nurse, Eli couldn't imagine what it would be like knowing this was the last time with his own ma. He wondered if cow years were like dog years and Little Joe was really almost grown and wouldn't mind being off on his own. But then Eli thought about Tater at four months. Tater was pretty tiny back then and still acted like a pup.

Eli unleashed Fancy so she could nuzzle her calf one more time. "You're a good mama," Eli said sweetly, stroking the hair between her eyes. She sniffed Eli's arm and snorted a warm breath of air into his elbow. "It'll be okay, Fancy," Eli said, not knowing if it was. "You'll have another baby to take care of next year. Grandpa will make sure of it."

Pa came back and took the lead strap off the hay bale. "Better get that halter back on," Pa told Eli. "After we take them down to the pastures, I'll get the pens cleaned up. Got a new batch of cow-calf pairs coming in. And you can pick out your show stall for E-1."

Pa hooked up Fancy. "Let me take her down to the pasture by the river maple first, then you follow with the calf." Fancy's hooves swished through the straw as Pa turned her around and led her out of the pen. "Be sure to keep your distance behind me."

Little Joe let Eli lead him to the pasture. Eli's hand was unsteady as the calf dipped down every other step to smell where Fancy had just been. But that's how it was with Little Joe. Now that the bull calf trusted him, Eli could pretty much lead the calf anywhere if Fancy wasn't too far away. And there were plenty of apples in Eli's pocket.

"Keep about five yards back," Pa hollered over his

shoulder. "I'll take her through the first gate, then out the other. E-1 won't even know what happened."

The pasture was crowded with steers. Eli could see them gliding in the field, chomping on new grass, and Old Gert in the middle, babysitting them all. They'd already cut into the clover on the top of the hill, mowing off the white tops, and were making their way down to fence level. Eli searched the heads and tails until he spotted the top of Fancy moving as she and Pa went through the first gate. Then more bodies and necks and hips. Eli wasn't sure who was who anymore. The cattle were all messed together—a jumble of tails drifting and rumps sitting. The sound of heads snorting as they munched.

"We're goin' out now!" Pa yelled. "To the pasture behind the fir trees, so don't follow. Get E-1 in. He won't even know she's gone."

Eli brought Little Joe into the pasture and put him beside Old Gert. The bull calf paused, sniffed at the ground and looked up. Then he trotted over to the second gate and started to bawl. "Come on out, son," Pa yelled. "Sooner or later he'll accept her being gone."

Eli put the apple slices on the ground and climbed through the fence. He watched as Little Joe ducked in and out of the herd searching for Fancy. The bull calf paced up and down the fence line between the two gates, coming back to the spots where he'd last smelled Fancy. All around him cattle grazed, tearing up green shoots to chew. But Little Joe didn't want a blade of grass. Or even the apple slices Eli'd left him. He wanted Fancy.

Eli stood quiet beneath the river maple. He didn't move when a cluster of maple keys spiraled down, nicking his cheek. He let the spinning wings scatter instead of picking them up like he'd done all the springs before, splitting them open and removing the seeds, then sticking the wings on his nose.

"School bus comes in fifteen minutes, Eli!" Ma had come down and was holding Eli's lunch. She dipped under the maple, pulled Eli close and kissed the top of his head. "You just keep growing, don't you?" Ma whispered. "But not too fast."

When Ma left, Eli reached out and touched the maple's peeling trunk. Brittle and gnarled, it still had strength. He leaned against it, closing his eyes until the sound of kids laughing came to him. Eli ran toward the laughter, following the orange hood of the school bus as it rounded the bend and stopped in front of Windswept Farms.

Eli lay in bed that night, wondering if he could ever be like Pa, snoring so hard no amount of calf bawling could wake him. Didn't Pa ever think about cows? *He won't even know she's gone.* That's what Pa'd said when Eli guided Little Joe to the pasture—snuck him in—like he said he'd never do again, fooling Little Joe with the smell of Fancy. Grandpa was right—Little Joe was bawling something awful. Eli could hear the calf wailing in the fields. He thought about Grandpa stroking Little Joe's head softly and then Eli's. Would Grandpa run out in the middle of the night and soothe Little Joe if he were his bull calf? That's what Eli wanted to do. He sat up and pulled off the covers but hesitated as he skimmed a toe across the floorboards. Grandpa didn't own Windswept Farms anymore. Pa did. And Pa'd told Grandpa they'd take care of things. Just him and Pa.

Eli blew out a gush of warm air, got back under the covers and tried lying still, not thinking about cows for once, but something else. Or nothing at all. For a few seconds the house was silent. *Maybe Pa can hear my bull calf bawling, too.* Eli lurched upright and grinned. But the snoring started up again. Pa had just turned over. He had no idea Little Joe was bawling into the night, aching for his ma.

"Can you hear it?" Hannah stood in Eli's doorway, tugging on a purple rabbit slipper.

"Hear what? Pa snoring?"

"Worse." She shuffled across the room.

"Shh. You'll wake up Ma and Pa," Eli warned.

"Ma can't sleep when Pa's snoring," Hannah said. "Help me up." She stuck out her polka-dot pajama arms. "Your bed's higher than mine and I've got slippers on."

"Ah, Hannah, there's barely enough room for Tater and me."

"Not if you scooch over."

Eli yanked both of Hannah's wrists and pulled her up.

"Something's crying," she whispered, pointing to the window looking over the pasture. "Out there."

"It's Little Joe." Eli sat up and brought his knees in close. "He's calling Fancy. They got split up today."

"What for?"

"'Cause it's time."

"But he's just a baby."

They both stopped and eyed the window. Little Joe's bawling had turned to a moaning so mournful it pierced the night with a new sadness.

"What are you gonna do?" Hannah asked.

"Pa says he'll accept her being gone soon enough."

"You can't listen to Pa. He doesn't like animals. Not the way you and me do."

"You sell your newborn rabbits out from under Snow White all the time."

Hannah bit her lip. "They go to good homes. And she always has a whole bunch more."

Then the rains came. Gushes so heavy they splashed

across the windowpanes, blurring anything Eli wanted to see outside.

"He doesn't have Spider out there, Eli. Or you."

"It's pouring rain."

Hannah rested her head on Eli's elbow. "You like rain."

It was true. In the summer Eli'd face the sky, open his mouth wide and taste the fat, warm raindrops caught on his tongue. When there was no school and wild blueberries to pick and nothing to worry about. Not like now, when it was ice-cold and damp and his bull calf was bawling.

"The slicker under my bed would fit you," Hannah said. "The one covered in rainbows."

"I'll be all right." Eli felt for his flashlight underneath the bed. Tater stood up and shook, then tiptoed around to where Eli'd been. He circled twice, slumped down into a ball and sighed, resting his chin on Hannah's stomach.

"Can I stay and snuggle with Tater?"

"If you don't go telling Pa I'm gone."

"I won't. I can keep a secret."

"And don't take my pillow."

A clap of thunder boomed so deep it crept into Eli's stomach. *One thousand. Two thousand. Three thousand*, Eli counted. *Four thousand. Five thousand.* Then another boom. *One mile away*, he thought. The thunder was getting closer. The light on the front porch flickered a few times, then finally sputtered out. Little Joe continued to cry. Slowly, Eli walked down the stairs, his fingers covering the beam of the flashlight so Pa wouldn't see. Then he put on his chore coat and headed for the fields.

The whites of Little Joe's eyes were showing when Eli reached the pasture. And he was wet. Sweaty coils of steam rose from his coat after all that mooing. On his own by the gate, the bull calf hung his head low as he bawled between muddy knees.

"There, boy," Eli murmured. He opened the gate and grabbed the halter. "Everything's okay."

But Little Joe's hair was so damp, Eli had a hard time gripping the halter. He decided to lead the bull calf with two hands and keep the flashlight in his pocket.

They headed up to the barn through a dark, wet thickness, Little Joe's bawl sounding more like a *baa* as they climbed. Eli was certain there wasn't a moon, but it was pouring too hard to look up. Every time he tried, heavy drops of rain caught Eli by surprise, making him blink back the sting.

When they got to the pen, there was no trace of Fancy. Or what had been. Pa'd bleached everything. The floors were stone gray and bare, except for the trickle of rain moistening a corner.

Eli put Little Joe in the pen anyway. The bull calf sniffed the bare walls and the manger where hay used to be. Eli hurried to the hay mow. He poked the hole in the ceiling hard with the butt of the hay fork to get some out. He ran with it to the pen and shook it over the floor.

Little Joe kept bawling.

Eli cut open a square of sawdust covered in plastic and shoveled that in, too.

Little Joe kept bawling.

Eli ran to the tack room to find something that smelled like Fancy. He grabbed a bunch of blankets and spotted the currycombs in a bucket.

Spider climbed to the top of the stanchion wall. She wrinkled the *M* on her forehead and yowled in between Little Joe's bawling as Eli spread the blankets over the pen.

Then Spider climbed down the wall to be with her calf.

"See this, boy?" Eli showed Little Joe the currycomb he'd brushed Fancy with.

For the first time, Little Joe stopped bawling.

Eli brushed Little Joe's poll with the comb, then the side of his neck, where the bull calf was still breathing heavy. "You should've never let me halter you," Eli said. "None of this would've happened." But Eli knew full well it would have. The next day. Or the next.

Exhausted, Little Joe closed his eyes and stopped fighting sleep. He let his front knees buckle, then his back legs, and got down on the ground and gave in to the night.

"Milkers don't spend half as long with their mothers." Eli spread his chore coat over Little Joe. "Not more than a few weeks. Sometimes one day. Maybe not even." Eli couldn't quite remember.

Spider licked Little Joe's eyelids.

"If you were a peeper, it'd be even worse. They don't even get to see their mamas. They're still jelly beans when they're left alone to hatch."

Little Joe rolled onto his side along the blankets.

"You're too big to nurse, anyhow," Eli said, resting his head on Little Joe's belly. He stretched out his arms, but the bull calf had grown beyond them.

Spider crawled under Little Joe's neck and purred, spinning herself tight against him like a ball of yarn.

She fell asleep first, then Little Joe and Eli, until the orange splinters of daybreak woke them up. The rain had stopped tapping on the barn roof. Eli could hear the sound of the bull calf's heart beating in his ear. "Guess we got our own story to tell," he whispered. "About the night you got weaned and it hurt so bad I stayed with you. And Spider, too. All night."

Little Joe's breath was softer now, and slower.

Eli figured there'd just be puddles outside, now that the rain was over. He could hear the birds again and the gutters gushing water. "I'll try and remember to tell you that story when we win the blue ribbon," Eli said. He could just imagine the silky blue prize pinned onto Little Joe's halter. "We will. You'll see." Eli stroked Little Joe's nose. "I promise. And this'll be your stall now. It'll get better from here on in."

All three of them were covered in sawdust when Pa came into the barn. Eli stumbled to his feet and shook off the bits of wood.

"What are you doin' here, son?"

Eli rushed to get the feed bucket outside the pen. "The calf keeps growin', Pa," he murmured. "Thought I'd feed him. In case there was a flood or something. On account of all that rain."

Pa craned his neck, looked up at the pen's ceiling, then kicked up some sawdust. "Looks dry to me," he said. "Listen. He's gotta learn to be on his own, Eli."

"But he's barely a teenager."

"Who told you that?"

"Grandpa."

Pa took his cap off, then put it back on. "Sounds like you're spending a whole lot of time talking and not enough on chores." Pa walked to the tack room and got out the spade, the one with the sharpest point. Eli knew what that meant. "Just 'cause you got a bull calf don't mean you can quit on your chores." Pa handed him the shovel. "It's time you dug up thistles."

"But I got school." The hair on Eli's arms bristled. He hated digging up thistles. And he was certain Pa knew it. Last year he got at least one bubbly blister from the wooden handle, and his eyes stung whenever a pricker whittled its way into the work gloves.

"Start with the pine fields, Eli. There's at least an hour before school."

Eli snatched the shovel away from Pa.

"Remember, slice the roots at least two inches below the soil to make it worthwhile. And don't go moving them. That'll just make the seeds spread."

"I've done it before," Eli hissed.

Pa swung around and stared hard at him.

"You showed me, Pa."

A sudden movement in the barn caught Pa's eye. He looked in the direction of the pen. Little Joe was peeking over the wall and blinking at him.

"You're gonna need a fan for that show stall," Pa said. "To keep him cool so his hair don't shed." Pa brushed some sawdust from Little Joe's neck with his hand. "We'll hang one up after school. Once you got the thistles done."

Chapter Nine

First Cut

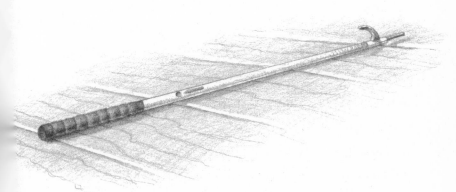

Grandpa took the show stick and lifted the pale green sheet. Eli knew what was under it. Every June since he could remember, Eli'd helped Grandpa get out Old Red, the trusty Farmall tractor, for the first hay cutting of the season.

"Still in mint condition," Grandpa said. He whistled, he was so pleased with the looks of Old Red. "The new ones just go faster and wear out quicker." Grandpa opened the hood. "These engines are simple. They don't go too fast and they don't go too slow. How much faster do you need to go in a field, anyhow?"

Eli stared at the glossy red tractor that had been kept

inside Grandpa's barn for nearly a year. "How old is Old Red now?" he asked.

"Let's see." Grandpa poked at a zigzag indentation digging deep into the white-rimmed tire. "My own pa used it when I was young, and he's been dead since I was ten. So Old Red's gotta be more than fifty years old."

Eli whistled, too. "A tractor can last that long?"

Grandpa tucked the show stick under his armpit. "A tractor should last at least a generation or two," he said. "Same as a show stick."

Grandpa handed the stick to Eli.

Eli's face grew warm as he examined the show stick. It was nearly as tall as he was and big as a golf club.

"Your pa took at least a dozen blue ribbons with that stick," Grandpa said, "coaxing and prodding his show animals in the big rings. It's yours now."

Eli clutched the silver part and eyed the glinting hooked tip. It was shaped like a bullet. He felt the sharp end with his finger and was surprised when it didn't hurt.

"I'll show you how to use it soon," Grandpa said. "Just like I did with your pa. It was his first show stick. Back when he had Shamrock."

"Shamrock." Eli liked saying it out loud. *So Pa did name his cattle. At least once, anyway.* "Was that Pa's first show animal?"

"Yep."

"Why'd he name her Shamrock?"

"'Cause she was born on Saint Paddy's Day."

Grandpa got out the gas can and started feeding its clear amber liquid to Old Red. "Oh, he did all sorts of fancy things for that heifer, I tell you. Got a green-colored halter for her and everything. He even sold eggs and live bait on the side of the road all summer just to pay for it."

"How'd they do?"

Grandpa capped the lid of the gas can and shifted his weight. But he didn't answer.

"At the fair, Grandpa?"

"That's a story for another time, Eli. Why don't you come take a look at my tomatoes?"

Eli followed Grandpa to the little tomato plot behind the barn, watching the metal on his show stick gleam whenever the sun caught it. He tapped the end of it on the checkered shell of a box turtle, crossing the old pasture to mate. Its shrivelly bald head disappeared inside the shell. Eli rested the show stick on his shoulder. It was heavier than he'd imagined, more like lugging a dozen eggs from the henhouse with one arm. He wondered if Little Joe would mind it and how easy it had been for Pa to line up Shamrock with it at one of the big shows. Maybe Shamrock didn't like it at all. If Grandpa didn't want to tell him about Shamrock, there must be a good reason, though Eli couldn't figure out why.

"They're budded up already, see?" Grandpa bent over a spindly green plant tied to an arrow with a rag. "This girl's starting a whole row of yellow flowers."

Eli looked to where Grandpa was pointing. The petals were pale as buttercups.

"Thanks to Saint Francis," Grandpa said, nodding over to the statue.

Ever since Grandma died, Grandpa's scarecrow in the middle of his garden was a clay likeness of Saint Francis of Assisi, Grandma's favorite saint. He stood two feet tall beside a rusty arrow now used as a stake, tilting his head and clutching a strand of rosary beads to his chest.

"Now I know it don't make much sense when you think about it at first," Grandpa admitted, rubbing the chipped toes peeking out of Saint Francis's coffee-colored robe, "since he's the patron saint of animals and all. And those are vegetables he's guarding. But if you think real hard, you can see it just plain makes sense. Saint Francis loves animals so much, they listen to him. And I mean all creatures. If he tells 'em not to eat my plants, they won't."

A crow who'd been sitting on the fence flew up and hovered around Saint Francis.

"See?" Grandpa cupped a palm over his eyes and squinted. "Never seen a crow yet land on Saint Francis. He gets 'em to keep their distance."

Grandpa tightened an old shoelace he'd tied around

the fence in case Saint Francis got too busy to keep the animals away. Then he started back to the barn. "Should we drive to Windswept Farms on Old Red?" Grandpa asked, waiting for Eli to catch up. "Or are you too old to sit on your grandpa's lap for the ride?"

Eli didn't care if he was too old. He headed to the farm on Grandpa's knee, watching Old Red's pipe belch up dark clouds of smoke. The engine rattled and hummed, and neither said much between the belching. They both knew this would be the last time. It would be Hannah's turn next year.

"Look!" Grandpa took a hand off the wheel and pointed to a mother deer and her fawn at the edge of the forest. "First time out." Grandpa smiled at the little fawn, not much bigger than Spider, who paused to look at them. "She's so new she doesn't know to be scared yet." Still learning to walk, the fawn took a step, then hopped forward with her back legs, catching up to her mother's beckoning white tail.

When they got to the farm, Eli jumped off and Pa fastened the cutter to Old Red. The late-day sun had turned the sky a burning orange. Eli and Pa watched Grandpa in shadow as he guided the tractor up the path and disappeared into the fields of timothy.

Eli focused on the skyline where the grain tips met up with the clouds, waiting for Grandpa to surface. He listened for the sound of the tractor. Once he heard the chugging, it meant Grandpa and Old Red had turned around and were getting closer. Eli watched as they came into view, rising up the hill toward him. Round and round the cutter spun as Grandpa and Old Red paused before starting in on another row. As soon as the earth dipped down again, they'd vanish and be waist-deep in timothy once more. Eli followed the dark wisps of smoke from Old Red's silver pipe until they melted into the sherbet-colored sky.

"Next time Grandpa comes round, you be ready," Pa said.

"For what?" Eli looked up at Pa.

"For driving the tractor."

Eli swallowed hard and felt his hands go limp and sweaty. He'd always wanted to drive a tractor instead of just riding on one, but it seemed awful sudden.

"It's just for a ways," Pa added. "Old Red won't go over ten."

Grandpa waved Eli over. He and Old Red were idling at the edge of the last patch of timothy.

Eli hesitated for a moment, then felt his legs take him over to the fields toward Grandpa and Old Red.

"Come on up, son. He don't bite." Grandpa stuck out his hand and Eli took it. "I'll still be here. But you'll be the one shifting the gears. Ready to try a row?"

All Eli could do was nod. He felt Grandpa's fingers

over his, and they both clasped the black knob on the shift lever tight.

"Put it in first, son."

Eli looked down and shifted the gear to the number one. Just like that, Old Red responded, lurching forward. Eli could hear the rattling of the cutter's chains as they dragged behind them and smell the grassy scent of fresh-cut timothy. *Pa's watching*, Eli figured, guiding Old Red up the hill. *I wish Keller could see this, too. And Tess.*

"Time to turn," Grandpa instructed, leading Eli's fingers to the cutter handle. "Spin the wheel hard to the left."

A flock of hungry barn swallows dipped down to peck for insects Old Red had scattered. As soon as Eli got the tractor going in a new direction, the birds swelled up and down in waves, making frantic sounds, fluttering their wings skyward.

When Eli had gotten through, Ma and Hannah were standing by Pa, watching. Grandpa shut off the engine and Hannah came running.

"Did you really drive Old Red by yourself, Eli?" she asked.

Eli nodded and climbed down just as Hannah screamed. He eyed a snake, hungry for any mice scrambling out of the empty fields. "It's just a corn snake," Eli said, watching the bright yellow bands on the snake's

As soon as Eli got the tractor going in a new direction, the birds swelled up and down. . . .

brown skin slither past. But Hannah was already back on the grass, hiding behind Ma.

"Good thing you'll be standing in the hay wagon when we bale," Eli hollered, nudging the six-foot snake with his boot tip to make sure it went the opposite way. Last year, Eli was the one standing in the hay wagon doing the stacking. Now he was big enough to toss the rectangular bales into the wagon, or at least up to Pa.

"Come here, son," Pa said, putting his arm over Eli's shoulders. "I wanna show you something."

Eli didn't think the evening could get any better than it was. A tent caterpillar dropped down from the bordering crab apple trees and wriggled its hairy spine across Eli's shirt sleeve. And the stars had come out, shiny and white as if the biggest moonflowers had decided to bloom right in the sky.

Pa walked Eli across the lawn to the other fields, where the corn grew. "Right here." He pulled back a vine, lime green and prickly, and showed Eli a pumpkin.

"She's a five-lober." Pa beamed. "The nicest I've had. And she's got the room." Pa pointed to the main vine. "She's ten feet out on a sixteen-foot main."

The pumpkin had already grown big as a baseball and was the color of creamed corn. Eli had to admit, she was a beauty. And big for this stage.

"I'm one step ahead of Ned Kinderhoff," Pa said,

uncovering a plastic bottle. He gave it a squeeze. Creamy white liquid squirted out. "It's milk," Pa said. "And not the pasteurized kind you get at the store . . . *real* milk." Pa dabbed his fingers with it, then coddled the leaf around the tiny pumpkin like it was a bitty baby bird, just hatched. "Kinderhoff's fancy glass greenhouse won't help him this year." Pa stroked the cut in the vine where the milk got fed through. "I'm gonna beat him. No more red ribbons. This time, the color will be blue." Pa turned to face Eli. "I got a way to speed things up with E-1, too. Boost his rations with corn silage and molasses."

Eli looked down at the pale-skinned pumpkin, its skin a waxy cream because of the milk. He sure hoped Pa would beat Ned Kinderhoff in the giant pumpkin division this year. He knew it'd be a first. But Eli didn't want to go rushing Little Joe. Last time he did, he got dragged through the mud. And Pa agreed Little Joe's rate of gain was higher than most. Three pounds a day! The valley was already talking about how impressive the calf looked. Grandpa thought the calf was plenty big enough, too, and better off on grass.

"But you said Little Joe's weight was fine, Pa. And Grandpa says calves fed on pasture are the healthiest."

Pa covered up the vine with some dirt. "Ned's got an eye on that calf, and he likes 'em big and meaty."

Eli didn't want to hear it. He wished he was out on a

log, just like those noisy bullfrogs, swelling up their yellow throats and croaking loud as they could. Or burying themselves in the mud whenever they felt like it.

"He's got money to burn, Eli. The more weight on that calf, the better. You get paid by the pound. Kinderhoff will bid whatever he wants if he sees a calf he likes."

Eli didn't want Ned Kinderhoff buying Little Joe. Ned Kinderhoff made Pa work late on payday, so Ma had to wait an extra day to go to the store. And he wore a belt buckle with shiny stones on it that you couldn't buy around here. When Eli saw Ned Kinderhoff at the fair last year, he walked into the show barn with sticky gray hair, clutching that fancy belt and wearing a smile that looked glued on.

"Wouldn't it be something," Pa said, "if we both had the biggest entries at the fair?"

Chapter Ten

Trading Eggs

Ma was in Sassy Clippers washing a new batch of eggs in the hair sink. "Look how big my hens are laying." Ma held up an egg to show Eli. It was peppered with chocolate-brown spots and nearly the size of a pear.

"I'll have that one for breakfast." Eli smiled. He stuck his index finger next to the egg, but the egg was longer.

"Sunny-side up or over easy?" Ma asked. She placed the egg in a measuring cup above the sink.

"Sunny-side up," Eli decided. "So I can see the size of the yolk." Eli climbed up the slippery black chair at the other hair sink and reached for the egg. It was surrounded by plastic bottles with pointy tops like in the condiment caddy at the Hoagie Hut. Only the colors in these didn't seem real. They were purple and orange and a metallic red that got used up every Saturday on a group of ladies. They waited outside—the old milk house wasn't meant to hold more than a milk tank—for their heads to get squooshed by a goosey-fleshed skullcap. Then Ma would take her crochet needle, weave it through the tiny pin-feather pricks in the cap and pluck. Whatever stuck out, Ma squirted with the color from the bottles. She smeared the mess around using a paintbrush before sending those ladies under the blower to roast.

Eli still couldn't believe Ma got paid for it.

"It'll only be a few minutes, Eli. Just one more rinse with cold water and the eggs will be clean."

"How come you're washing them up so nice?" Eli wondered. "It's only us."

Ma turned redder than the bottle of hair dye. "All these eggs aren't for us, Eli." Ma patted down the eggs with a towel. "They're for my clients."

"You mean you give the extras away?"

"No. Not exactly." Ma pointed to the window. "Could you hand me one of those cartons by the windowsill?"

Eli sat down on the vinyl chair, reluctant to move. "But Pa says we don't sell eggs."

"They're my hens," Ma said. She walked over and got

a carton herself. "Besides, I don't sell my eggs; I trade them. For other things."

"Won't Pa be sore when he finds out?"

"I don't interfere with the cattle and he doesn't meddle with my hens. For the most part. I do what feels right, Eli, and I don't always tell your pa. You need new roper boots for the fair and a new blower to groom Little Joe." Eli went and got another carton by the window and started in on a dozen eggs.

"I figure twenty-four more dozen eggs to Mrs. Krueger till we get them. She always comes down from the Agway and asks for two dozen on Mondays." Ma winked at Eli. "Hand me that marker by the talcum brush, will you? And write down her name on this one." Ma handed Eli the full carton.

"How do you spell *Krueger*?" They both laughed, and Ma pointed to Mrs. Krueger's name on the first dozen. "You know your pa's not as bad as all that, Eli. He just saves his caring for when it matters."

"Grandpa says we got enough caring to go around for everyone. Animals, too."

"Your pa's a good farmer, Eli."

"Then how come he likes pumpkins over cows?"

"I guess pumpkins don't hurt." Ma opened the old Frigidaire and laid her dozen on the stack labeled EXTRA

LARGE. "How 'bout some buttermilk pancakes to go with that gigantic egg?"

"With peach maple syrup on top?"

"I think we still have some left." Ma smiled. She handed Eli his giant egg and they walked out of the old milk house toward the kitchen.

Chapter Eleven

Cow Tipping

Eli lay on his bed not knowing what to do. He stared at the soldiers on the papered walls that had been there since Grandpa was a boy. But Eli was too angry to concentrate on which clusters of military men carried swords and which ones had bayonets slung over their shoulders. He was mad about the rain.

"You sure they canceled the fireworks, Pa?" Eli yelled. He leaned forward, clasped his arms around his knees and looked outside. It hadn't even sprinkled yet.

Pa came into the room, tucked his hands into his jean pockets and peered through the window. "Sure looks like rain," Pa said.

The clouds hung low, gathering strength near the barn.

They were stained blueberry, the edges a deep watermelon, same as a bruise.

"They're tryin' to figure out what to do," Pa said. "If hot or cold's gonna win out."

Eli figured hot would. It had been the hottest Fourth of July he could remember. His rocket Popsicle had melted before he'd gotten to the white part, watching the parade that afternoon. Even now, Eli was waiting for the fan to blow in his direction and keep his bangs from sticking to his forehead.

"You check the fields?" Pa asked, angling his chin to catch a glimpse of the pastures. "Lupine's in season. Lobelia, too." Pa'd skimmed his cheek toward the window so close it was almost touching. "The stems'll be sapping up now. If they've grown at all."

Eli had already checked Little Joe's pasture. He'd scoured the rocks for any spiky flowers blooming cone-like that might be lupine, careful not to step into a steaming mound of cow manure the damp heat refused to harden. He'd examined each flowering plant growing wild in tufts along the hillside. It didn't matter if they weren't white or pink or blue. Eli checked them anyhow, until beads of sweat collected on his nose and the sun made his head ache. But it was always the same. Nothing was ever lupine. Lobelia, either.

Pa'd showed him all the poisonous plants a cow could

get sick on in the seed catalog so many times, Eli wondered if that was the only place they'd ever bloomed. And this afternoon, his legs were just too tired to walk down to Fancy's field, where all the pregnant cows grazed. Eli'd seen them high up by the pines, standing in the shade. They hadn't even chewed the cud yet. It was so hot, they rubbed their necks and chins against each other to scratch away the face flies. Besides, he'd just combed the field last week for any purple flowers. There were none.

"Still time before it rains." Pa cleared his throat. "And gets too dark." He headed out the door.

It was almost dusk when Eli walked toward Fancy's field, but it hadn't cooled down yet. He took his wrist and wiped the beads of sweat lining his brow. The trees had gone dark before the sky did, sticking out their inky branches against the purple smudge of clouds. Encouraged by the heat, the katydids kept calling, scraping their wings together so loudly Eli had to remind himself the insects weren't any bigger than his pinky finger.

"You a cow yet?"

Eli swiveled toward the voice and spotted Keller on the creek path, wet from a swim.

"Figured you must've become part of the herd, since I never see you around." Keller smiled. He yanked the T-shirt hanging from the back of his jeans and swatted a knee.

"Horsefly," he said. "Bite straight through anything." Keller pulled the T-shirt over his head, which had been shaved.

"What happened to your head?" Eli pointed at Keller's shiny skull. He could see a whole bunch of nick marks forming lines smudged red.

"Too hot to have hair on it," Keller said. "Got in the way of the sweat, so I shaved it."

It was almost dark by now and impossible to make out colors on anything blooming.

"That's where you were going, wasn't it?" Keller asked. "To see if the cows were fartin' the right way?"

"No." Eli scowled. It was bad enough that Keller had swum in *his* creek. "I was gonna check for lupine or anything poisonous they could get into," he told Keller.

"Lupine?" Keller bulged out his eyes and laughed. "The only thing growing through these rocks is weeds. Don't matter if it rains or not."

They both looked up at the sky and felt nothing but hot air.

"There's other Fourth of July traditions besides fireworks," Keller said, rubbing a palm against his skull. "Come on."

"Where are we going?" Eli jogged to keep up.

"Cow tipping." Keller threw Eli a picket fence smile before hopping over the barbed wire to the pasture where Little Joe grazed.

Eli froze.

"Aw, come on," Keller said. "Everybody does it. I bet your pa did it when he was young, too."

Not Pa, Eli thought. Pa never spent more time with his cattle than he needed, but he'd named his first calf Shamrock. Bought her a green halter and everything. And Eli couldn't imagine tipping anything, let alone Little Joe. You tipped on a Tilt-A-Whirl at the fair or leaning over to pick up a stray bale of hay off Grandpa's tractor. You tipped over a rain barrel if the mosquitoes got to it. You tipped over when you needed to, not because you wanted to.

"They're just a bunch of stupid cows." Keller stuck out his arms like he was sleepwalking or a robot. Then he knelt on all fours and began to moo.

"They . . . they ain't stupid," Eli stammered, climbing through the fence real gentle. He didn't want to go startling them. And he didn't want Keller running loose with *their* cows. Keller had tipped over plenty of things—burn barrels and beehives—kicked them, too. Feed buckets and oil cans, hay wagons and outhouses. Just for fun. Eli knew Keller would tip over Little Joe and not think twice about it.

"Don't tell me you've gone and fallen in love with them." Keller grinned. "Betcha give 'em a good-night kiss, too. Kissy, kissy!" Keller puckered up his lips and inched closer to Eli's face.

Eli pushed Keller away and focused on the shadows. The cows looked different at night. Whenever the moon cut through the muddy sky, it cast a shimmer over the cattle. Their hides gleamed like dragonfly wings. Eli heard belching and burping and munching. Most of the cross-breds were resting on the ground, chewing their cud, eyes glassy and dark as marbles staring back at him. *Good*, Eli thought. *If they're all lying down, they can't get tipped over.*

"No need to worry, lover boy. It don't hurt them." Keller was whispering now and crouching low. "It's funny. You give one a push and boom! Down they go. Just like dominoes. Or a punching bag. Only they don't pop back up. It takes a while for them to get to their feet again, but they do."

Eli spotted a gray muzzle grasping the bottom branch of an oak tree with a tongue to get at the leaves. He thought it was Little Joe. But then Eli caught a flash of white, jagged as a puzzle piece in the middle of the hide.

"Ain't that your calf over there?" Keller asked, pointing past the tree.

Eli knew the topline straightaway. It was Little Joe. He'd trimmed the calf's rump hairs that morning. Now the perfectly groomed tailhead was facing them, straight as an arrow. He was standing next to Old Gert and they both looked awful quiet. As if they might be sleeping.

"Whatcha gonna do when he goes and gets sold on you at the fair? Cry like a baby? Boo hoo!" Keller fisted up his hands and rubbed both eyes. "Wouldn't the judges love that. Take away your ribbon, I bet."

Move! Eli thought, watching Keller creep closer to Little Joe. Instead, a firefly snapped, bursting light into the air before becoming invisible again.

Keller craned his neck and looked behind his shoulder. "I'll show you how it's done," he mouthed, reaching over to tap Little Joe's hip.

Eli tackled Keller and Little Joe bucked up. The two boys tumbled down the pasture in a tangle until a rock jutting out of the hillside stopped them. A corn snake getting warmed by the heat of the stone slithered across Keller's waist. Keller bolted upright and let out a scream—high-pitched—just like a girl's. *Just like Hannah*, Eli thought.

"It's just a corn snake!" Eli laughed.

The herd galloped down the hill in a circle, then came back to look at Eli, surrounding them both. Little Joe edged closer and sniffed Eli's head.

"Don't tell me you're afraid of snakes, Keller. Ain't that something?"

"Am not!" Keller brushed off his belly to make sure the snake hadn't left anything on it. "I didn't see it coming, that's all."

Old Gert had settled down, her legs tucked under. She was making a crunching sound, moving her lips sideways in opposite directions, chewing her cud. Keller knelt and leaned against her, then looked down at the grass and decided to stand.

"How you gonna cow tip if you're afraid of snakes?" Eli teased.

Fireworks exploded into the sky, peppering the darkness with streaks of orange and blue and white. The herd did another loop around the pasture, waiting for Old Gert to catch up before stopping.

"Guess they're doing the fireworks anyway," Keller hollered, looking up at the globes of cascading color. "Maybe we'll cow tip another night. When it's not the Fourth of July."

"Nah." Eli shook his head. "You wouldn't want me messing with your Sour Patch pigs, would you?"

Keller stuck his hands in his pockets, shrugged his shoulders and spit.

Then they both eyed the shadowy outlines of the cattle as they galloped farther down the hillside.

Eli was heading for the house when he heard splashing in the creek. He went down and saw Pa and Hannah swimming.

"Where you been?" Pa asked, stroking toward the bank.

"Checking on the cattle."

"It's dark, son." Pa stopped swimming and wiped the water from his eyes. "Has Keller been gettin' you to cow tip?"

"Nah." Eli shook his head. *How did Pa know about that?*

Pa came up on the bank and swatted a mosquito above Eli's head. "The Tibbets do that every Fourth. Never saw much point in it. A calf could get hurt. Bruise its flesh."

A few fat raindrops fell on their shoulders. Pa looked up at the sky.

"There's something I've been meaning to show you for a while, son." Pa held back a few dripping bangs. "And I better hurry. Now it's something big." Pa smirked, walking backward. "So you better stand clear." Then he turned around, sprinted toward the creek and pitched into the air.

"Cannonball!" Hannah shouted, watching Pa grab hold of his knees.

Pa shattered the surface of the swimming hole with a big fat cannonball.

"You try it, Eli!" Hannah laughed.

"The only way to get the mosquitoes off ya is to go under," Pa said.

"I got my clothes on."

"But you're already wet," Hannah pointed out.

It was raining harder now. Warm drops dribbled down Eli's nose.

Eli took off his sneakers and socks. The ground was just softening. When he looked up, Pa and Hannah had cleared the way, bobbing in the water ten feet apart.

Eli's heart beat faster and he began to run. As he jumped, he could see Pa laughing and Hannah clapping. He hit the water with his shins hard and it smarted. But he was having too much fun to care. He went under the water and grinned.

Chapter Twelve

❧

In the Show Ring

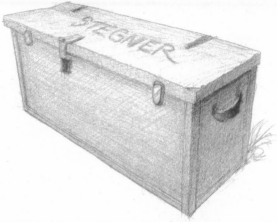

Little Joe didn't like to step over anything, especially not the garden hose obstacle Grandpa had coiled round, its shiny nozzle poking up like a copperhead snake in front of the silo. Eli clenched hard on the calf's halter. He pulled left, leading Little Joe around it and into the imaginary ring.

"Good. Now set him up," Grandpa commanded, pressing a finger against his nose and looking serious under his straw hat. "And pretend like I'm the judge," he added, fanning his face with the other hand. "You're in the show ring now, remember. The fair's not even two months away."

The three of them were already sweating. Smatterings of filmy cobwebs the outdoor spiders had spun overnight still hung like dew blankets over the lawn, and the daisies were just opening up. It was going to be another scorching August day. Eli wished he had a hat on, too, but you couldn't compete if you wore one.

Eli waited until the calf's front legs were straight before tugging on the lead strap to get him to stop. All he could hear was the soft tinkling of the chain on the leather strap. And crickets. They didn't even bother keeping quiet during the day anymore; it was just as hot at night.

"Hindquarters," Grandpa pointed out. "Calf posture's real important." He knelt down and leaned closer, examining the space between Little Joe's feet as if he could measure the distance in his head. "Get 'em wide to form a rectangle with them other legs."

Eli poked the tip of the show stick in the fleshy fold between Little Joe's toes to get him to move. Little Joe stepped a bit wider. Eli smiled.

"Seems he likes being shown off," Grandpa said, impressed by Little Joe's stance. "He's not fightin' it. And he's not fightin' you."

The first time Eli tried the show stick a few months ago, Little Joe kicked at it, thinking it might be a fly or some other kind of biter. But Eli worked with the calf every day, prodding his toes and dewclaws lightly with the stick, then pulling it away real quick whenever Little Joe lashed out. Once the calf saw there was nothing to be afraid of, he stopped kicking and started listening to Eli.

"A little too wide, Eli. Bring him back," Grandpa said. "Remember—the halter tells him where to go. The stick tells him which foot to move."

Eli took the hook of the stick and jabbed Little Joe's callused dewclaws with it. *Perfect*, he thought, keeping his gaze on the calf's poll as he obeyed. Eli stroked Little Joe's black belly. He'd gotten him perfectly lined up when Little Joe lunged forward, showing Eli the whites of his eyes as he stepped out of line. Eli looked around to spot the trouble. It was Tater. He'd found relief from the heat in a tractor divot the wheels had made in the muck.

"No fair, Grandpa," Eli moaned. "Tater spooked him!"

Tater rolled around in the murky water. He splashed his tail and showed his black gums until he sneezed from being upside down too long.

"That's good," Grandpa said. "Just like in a show ring." He grinned. "Animals doing what they want, when they want. Getting into trouble. Behaving as they please."

Eli pulled the currycomb from his back pocket and brushed the drool off Little Joe's neck. Then he scratched the calf s belly with the show stick to get him settled.

"It don't concern you," Grandpa told Eli, folding his arms and walking in a semicircle around Eli and Little Joe. "It's just the judge, you and Little Joe in that ring, far as you're concerned. Now tap him on the nose with the butt of the stick. That'll get him listenin'."

Spider walked under Little Joe while Eli was leading him around the ring. It didn't seem to bother Little Joe. Expertly, the two moved together, Spider weaving in between the calf's feet as he stepped a front hoof, then a back hoof, forward.

"Keep half a cow's length between you and them," Grandpa ordered, pointing at Spider. "And if you go past the water tub, you're out of the ring."

Eli held Little Joe back, waiting for Spider to trot away, careful to keep half a cow's length behind her. She lay low instead, stalking a pair of gingerbread-striped kittens with her yellow eyes. Eli turned Little Joe around near the tub before Spider chased the kittens down the hill.

"Good instincts, son. Always turn away from the trouble." Grandpa clasped his hands. "I'd say you're ready."

Eli wished he could show in his class right now.

Grandpa got out the soft strip of girth tape and wrapped it around Little Joe. "Forty-six inches," he called out, reading the tape measure. "Nice and meaty. I figure he's seven hundred pounds, and that's being modest."

Grandpa rolled up the tape, put it back in his pocket and smiled. "That's what good breeding and green pasture can do to a calf. Looks like you're both ready." Grandpa hauled the tub of water and fed it to Little Joe. "There's just one more thing I need to show you."

Eli couldn't imagine what else he needed to learn about posing.

"Get your bull calf back into the barn first. He's been out long enough. You don't want his hide getting red from too much sun."

Eli led the calf into his show stall and turned on the fan he and Pa'd hung from the ceiling. He hoped it would keep Little Joe cool enough to get his hair growing. He clawed at Little Joe's underbelly with his fingernails where the red patches were, forcing them to shed. Blue ribbon Anguses always had black hair that was thick and glossy. He'd have to keep Little Joe inside more during the day and let him out to graze at night so the sun wouldn't color more clumps red.

Eli turned on the radio dangling from the manger with binder twine so Little Joe could get used to other people's voices. He'd hear thousands of them at the fair.

"Come on out, son," Grandpa called.

Eli squinted to block out the sunlight and nearly tripped over the box in front of him.

"Can't show without a show box," Grandpa said.

Eli looked down and saw a shiny square box the size of a newborn calf. It was painted bright red. Even though the gold letters were upside down from where he stood, Eli knew they spelled STEGNER.

"Figured your birthday's comin' up after the fair and

it's a long ways before Christmas, so it makes sense to give you this early."

Eli'd seen them at shows before. In catalogs, too. They were expensive. Especially nice ones. This one had leather handles on each end that looked brand-new.

"Go ahead. Open it," Grandpa urged, swinging the box around on its wheels to face Eli.

Eli unclasped the shiny silver latches and looked inside. There was everything you could imagine in the way of showmanship: Sullivan's livestock shampoo, clippers and combs and shoe polish to darken Little Joe's hooves.

"It's mostly new," Grandpa began, "the things in there. Like the spray cans of show gloss to make 'em look pretty. The old stuff's from when your pa showed."

Eli kept staring, drinking in the notion that it was all his. Spider scurried over to take a peek and hopped inside, wrapping her tail around the edge of the lid.

"This was his currycomb." Grandpa pulled out a soft brush. "That's for good luck, you know."

Eli took the comb and studied it. *This was in Pa's pocket when he showed*, Eli thought. *When he won the blue ribbons*. He took out the comb that was already in his back pocket and replaced it with Pa's.

"I'll tell you another thing that's ready," Grandpa said, clearing his throat. He walked to his truck and brought out some bright red fruit. "It's my tomatoes."

Grandpa had left a tip from the vine on the one he handed to Eli. Eli plucked it free and took a bite, taking in the peppery smell that clung to his fingers.

Tater bounded over and barked at the show box before nudging his face into Eli's hand, itching for a taste, too.

"It takes two people to lift that box into the show barn, Eli," Grandpa said. "Your pa on one end, you on the other. Remember, I'll be with you in that show ring, whether I'm really in there or not."

Eli gave Tater the rest of the tomato and looked up at Grandpa. Now his hands were free to give him a hug.

Chapter Thirteen

Poison Weeds!

Little Joe stuck his neck over the fence as far as it could go. He flicked his gray tongue in the air like a lizard, snatching a branch with it.

"Not too many apples down that low," Eli told him.

A fistful of crumpled leaves fluttered into Little Joe's face.

Eli rattled a high branch with both hands to get some apples to drop. A few lumpy ones rolled to the ground on his side of the fence. Eli scooped up two and steadied them in his palm. What Little Joe liked most this time of year were sour green apples freckled with brown spots right out of Eli's hand. Little Joe's mouth felt like warm rubber grabbing onto Eli's fingers, but he never bit.

The wind blew heavy, drowning out Little Joe's crunching. It played shadow with the sun between the maple trees, washing over Little Joe's coat with ripply waves of dark and light. Eli looked up at the tops of the maples, where the gusts grew stronger. Caught in the teeth of the wind, their branches bobbed back and forth, trying to keep the early autumn leaves from blowing away. But they spun around like pinwheels, faster and faster, until they let go, sending a shower of color down on Little Joe.

"Eli!"

The wind carried Pa's shout over the hillside. *Something's wrong.* Eli knew it from the way Pa sounded.

Eli dropped the apple he was feeding Little Joe and raced up the field. It was harder going up the hill than running down it. He was out of breath within a few strides and slipped on a pile of leaves. Scrambling to his feet, Eli scared the wild turkeys into flying off. He focused on the space where the hill broke and became flat, sucking in more air while he ran against the wind. The closer Eli got, the tighter his chest became. When he was halfway up the hill, he could see Pa standing at the top, one arm splayed out against the sun, dangling something lifeless in his fist.

"What's wrong, Pa?" Eli burst out, breathless.

"This." Pa's face had turned the color of birch bark. He showed Eli what was in his hand.

Now Eli could see what Pa was holding. A clump of

lobelia, roots hanging from Pa's fingers, clotted with dirt. "When was the last time you checked the fields?" he boomed.

This morning, Eli thought. But yesterday felt the same as today. And the days before. His mind raced through the weeks, stretching to remember when he'd searched the fields last. But it was all a blur. *Which field was it and when?* Eli was never good at days. There was no school in summer, so every day seemed like a Saturday. Now that school had started up again, Eli hadn't paid much attention to flowers and weeds. He'd been too busy gearing up for the fair.

"Yesterday," Eli finally spat out. "Or the day before." But he knew it wasn't true. Eli's legs grew wobbly and his throat was bone dry.

"Couldn't have." Pa stared coldly at Eli. "It's good and bloomed. I found it in the field where the mother cows are. No telling if the crossbreds might've eaten it. Or Fancy. Who knows how their calves will come out." Pa turned away from Eli. "Won't know till spring."

Eli had to sit down. He knew his legs wouldn't support him much longer. He'd seen pictures of what happened when cow mothers ate poisonous plants. Pa'd showed him a photo last year of a tiny calf with front legs all crooked, her bones so brittle she could barely walk.

"Didn't I tell you to check the fields every day?"

Eli felt a rush of sadness wash over him. He tried to sniff back the tears, but they welled up in his eyes anyway.

Pa took out a lighter and torched the root ends. He held on until the clump became a ball of fire. Then Pa tossed the burning plant to the ground and stomped it with his boots. "I've got a mind to ground you from showing at the fair, Eli," he said. "Because of what you done."

"No!" Eli's voice exploded. "You can't do that, Pa!" he cried, choking back tears.

"You'd still get the money." Pa's hands were trembling. Eli'd never seen him this way. "Ned'll buy your calf, anyhow." Pa kept squashing the plant with his boots, but it was already a shriveled heap of stringy black bits.

Money? Eli hadn't even thought of the money. He had to get away. He sprinted into the barn and kicked at his show box hard before slipping into the empty pen. He slumped down into the straw and let the tears flow.

How had he forgotten to check the fields? *What if one of them babies comes out crooked?* It would be his fault. And there was nothing he could do about it.

Eli pulled himself up and leaned against the stone wall of the foundation to keep his head from spinning. *I'm not even going to get a shot at winning the blue ribbon*, he thought. Eli slid down the wall slowly, hoping the coolness would soothe him, but it didn't. He crouched down, curling his knees up close, and cried some more.

Eli slid down the wall slowly, hoping the coolness would soothe him, but it didn't.

"There you are." Grandpa stood over the gate to the empty pen.

"I—I didn't mean to forget, Grandpa," Eli stammered. "Really I didn't. I know I checked the fields. Just not yesterday. And maybe not the day before."

"Ah, son. It's not your fault." Grandpa opened the gate and slid down into the straw, too. Eli opened his eyes and looked up at him. Shafts of light streamed across Grandpa's shoulder, carrying flecks of dust from the straw bedding.

"I saw the lobelia," Grandpa said. "It wasn't even chewed on. And you didn't make it grow." He lifted Eli's chin. "They can bloom in an afternoon, anyhow. Now help me up."

"I won't win the blue ribbon," Eli said as soon as he saw the show box. "Pa said I can't go to the fair 'cause it's all my fault."

"Will you stop carrying on like that? You can't know the pasture every minute of the day. Now quit your sniveling and start listening. It ain't your fault, you hear me?" Grandpa repeated. "A cow'd have to eat a whole lot of lobelia to have a calf come out crippled."

Grandpa stroked the top of Eli's head. "I'm gonna tell you something, not because I want you to feel worse, but because I want you to know about your pa." Grandpa pulled Eli onto the show box next to him. "I told you your pa's first show animal was Shamrock, didn't I? Back when your pa was a boy. About your age."

Eli sniffed, then nodded, wiping his wet nose with the back of his hand.

"What I didn't tell you is what happened to her." Grandpa gripped a corner of the show box with his fingers before letting out a deep breath. "Things were goin' real good with the training. Shamrock was always good on the training part. She was so attached to your pa with all the fussin' he gave her, she'd do anything he asked. Trusted him wholeheartedly. One hundred percent. But she was lean on the weight, see?" Grandpa jabbed at the middle of his glasses. "I didn't care much, but your pa did. He wanted to win that blue ribbon so bad, he thought if he grazed her on fresh pasture loaded with clover she'd bulk up some and her backbones wouldn't stick out as much."

Grandpa rubbed the side of his face with a callused-up hand. "We didn't have any fresh pastures—not enough land to rotate the fields each season—so he took her over to old Rupert's fields, which hadn't been chewed on in years. I didn't even know about it till it was too late."

Eli leaned forward and stared at Grandpa. "Too late for what, Grandpa?"

"The field was peppered with lupine, son. And she was all alone in the pasture. With no grown cows like Old Gertie or Fancy to show her not to. She was dead the next day. Must've eaten a whole lot. Your pa was heartbroken. Didn't talk for days. Still don't talk much."

Now Eli knew why Pa's heart had dried up. And why he acted the way he did when he found the lobelia. Eli felt another rush of emotion well up into his throat, this time for Pa. He'd make sure to check the fields twice a day from now on. Even after blooming season was over. *Until the first snowfall,* Eli decided. He wanted to run to Pa and tell him how sorry he was about Shamrock. He wouldn't even care if Pa hugged back. But he was afraid to.

"I'll talk to your pa," Grandpa whispered. "Just because he didn't get to show at the fair that first year doesn't mean you shouldn't. That was then. Now it's your turn, son."

Eli hoped Grandpa could convince Pa, but he knew how different they were. "Pa says we talk too much."

"He does? Well, I got a right to be with my grandson. Tell him a few things." Grandpa pulled Eli closer, the way he always did. Eli couldn't help but smile.

"You and Pa sure are different," Eli said.

"Your pa's got a particular way of seeing things, Eli. It don't have to be yours. If you don't want it to."

But Eli wanted to please Pa. Whenever he caught sight of the winning photos in the tack room, his neck hairs tingled. And he figured if he got close enough to winning the blue ribbon with Little Joe, Pa might be proud of him.

"You *are* gonna lose him, son."

"Huh?" Eli leaned over to look at Grandpa.

"Your show animal."

Eli wasn't ready to think about that.

"Sometimes nature decides when, sometimes a cattle sale does." Grandpa put an arm around Eli. "That's just the way it is. Doesn't mean you stop caring just because it hurts. If you do, you turn away all the good that comes from knowing them. The only thing sadder than losing a show animal is hardening up for good."

Chapter Fourteen

❧

No Trespassing

Eli started off slowly beside the nodding white petals of Queen Anne's lace, dawdling along the gravel shoulder next to the road that led to Tess's farm. He wanted to see the horses. He'd been told more foals had been born and hoped to touch them before they got too big. Maybe he'd see Tess. Tess was different. She wasn't always talking like Hannah. And she was close to her horses the way he was to his calf without ever having to say it. Eli didn't feel like saying much. Or thinking. Especially about what Grandpa had told him in the barn. Or the lobelia Pa found in Fancy's field.

Eli tugged at his cap and began to jog as soon as he heard whinnying. When he got near the white ribbons on the electric fence surrounding the pastures, Blue barked.

"Blue! Come here, Blue!" It was Tess calling. The little blue-gray dachshund waddled next to her heels with his squatty legs and stuck out his tongue.

Eli rested behind the deeply grooved trunk of a sugar maple nearly stripped of its golden leaves and caught his breath. He watched Tess lead an Appaloosa he hadn't seen before into the pasture above the lake.

"Hi, Eli." Tess smiled. Eli looked around the tree and smiled, too.

Tess took off the twine holding the pasture gate in place and guided the speckled horse through it. She unhooked the lead chain and the horse galloped free, kicking and bucking at the wind. He slowed to a trot and flared his nostrils when he got close to the others and saw they were grazing.

"Come to see the babies?" Tess asked.

"Uh-huh."

"They're in the pasture by the lake where it's nice and flat. No gopher holes. And no electric fence to zap them. Come see."

They watched the foals frolicking in the fields and rolling around in the last patches of clover. Eli marveled at their long, spindly legs. They splayed out in all directions, yet somehow the foals didn't topple over.

"Their mouths are softer than velvet," Tess whispered.

A tan one bit the neck of another to get him to play.

They galloped away with bushy tails in the air so new, the stubs barely covered their rumps.

Tess climbed through the fence and made a clucking sound. Two foals came over. She took a cloth from her back pocket and wiped their eyes with it.

"Still fly season," she told Eli. "And their tails are too short to shoo anything away." Tess curled an arm around the neck of the rust-colored one and guided him toward the fence. "Would you like to touch him?"

"Sure."

The colt's black mane stood straight up and was all feathery. *Just like a toothbrush*, Eli thought. *Only not near as many bristles*. Eli could see right through it.

"Go ahead. Reach your hand out, palm flat, and he'll sniff it," urged Tess.

Eli stretched out his arm too quickly. The foal got spooked and backed away.

"They're so skittish at this age," Tess said. "Try again. Give me your hand this time and I'll bring it to him."

Tess took Eli's palm and rested it on top of hers. Slowly, she guided it toward the colt. He didn't get spooked and sniffed at Eli's fingers. Snorting out a warm breath of air, the colt skimmed Eli's palm with his mouth.

"It is soft." Eli smiled. Tess was right. It was softer than velvet. Softer than anything Eli'd ever touched. He imagined it must be even softer than the velvety skin he'd seen hanging off a buck's antlers. And it was softer than the pinkest part on Tater's belly.

Tess laughed and studied the colt like Eli studied Little Joe. She examined his legs, cupping her hand around a tiny ankle and sliding it up the tendon. "They're pretty helpless when they're babies," she said, feeling a scab below the colt's knee. "They need lots of attention."

Tess picked some straw out of his mane in the same gentle way Ma used to comb Eli's hair when he was little. She ran her fingers through his stringy mane and the colt stepped on Tess's foot. She giggled and looked down at the hoof, no bigger than a few fingers. "They go barefoot until they become yearlings," Tess explained. "Then they get shoes on the front feet."

Eli stuck a sneaker under the fence. The little hooves were the color of his shoelaces. "Cows don't get anything done with their hooves till they're at least a year old," Eli mentioned, happy he knew that.

"Oh. I didn't know that. Is your calf a year old?" Tess asked.

"He'll be a little over nine months at the fair."

"When do you show?"

"Tomorrow." *If I even go*, Eli thought. He kept eyeing the colt's hooves, trying not to think about the fair.

"I could never do that." Tess climbed under the fence and stood beside Eli.

"Do what?"

"Part with an animal the way beef farmers do." She shook away a loose brown hair from her forehead. "I couldn't imagine taking care of an animal every day, then going to the fair and selling it. None of us in my family could."

"It's different with beef farmers," Eli admitted. He thought of Pa and how he kept growth charts filled with numbers on all the crossbreds. And how he even *named* them numbers. Eli could never do that. *I'd have to give them real names*, he thought. *Just like I did with Little Joe.*

"Don't you want to win a blue ribbon?" he asked Tess.

"Oh, I've got plenty of ribbons," she said. "Not to brag or anything. I go to competitions all the time with Chili Pepper. She's grazing up there." Tess pointed to the paddock where the older horses were. "I always get nervous. Don't know why. I do the same jumps with her down by the lake a hundred times, but the minute I enter the show ring, I forget. Only for a second, though. Chili Pepper reminds me. She helps me win all the time."

Tess swung around and leaned into the rail to face Eli. "Is it like that with Little Joe? Does he help you, too?"

Eli thought about his calf and smiled. "He's just a big old teddy bear." Eli laughed. "Once he got used to me leading him around. And he'll do anything I ask him to. Poses like he's a movie star. As long as Tater don't spook him."

"I bet you'll win," Tess said. "Then you'll get lots of money to buy another one." She paused, then forced out a laugh. "Guess I'm lucky they don't eat horses and I can keep mine each year."

"Yes, they do." Keller had snuck up from behind. Both Tess and Eli jumped a little from the fence.

"They eat horses over in Europe," Keller said. "That's where my grandma's from." He tried to squeeze into the space between Tess and Eli. "They make glue out of 'em, too. That's why glue smells the way it does."

"I don't believe it." Tess hopped onto the lower rail and whistled at a foal that skittered by.

Eli didn't believe it, either.

"Has your brother fixed that halter yet?" Keller asked, tapping the back of Tess's shoulder.

"Oh yeah," Tess said, climbing down from the rail. "I'll go and get it."

They both watched Tess as she headed to the barn.

"You got a halter that needs fixin'?" Keller asked Eli.

Eli shook his head.

"Then what are you here for?"

"To see the horses," he mumbled.

"Yeah, and who else?"

Eli turned red and set his gaze across the pasture.

Tess came back and handed Keller the halter. All three of them just stood there, not knowing what to say.

Keller stared down at Eli. "Finished seeing the horses yet?"

Eli pulled the brim of his cap lower and followed Keller to the road.

"Good luck at the fair, Eli!" Tess called out.

"Good luck at the fair, *Ee-lie*!" Keller mimicked, making his voice sound dumb and squeaky.

"Your calf ready?" Keller asked, breaking the silence that had come between them as they walked along the road from Tess's.

"Guess so." Eli wasn't about to tell Keller that he might not be going to the fair. "How's your pigs?"

"Same as ever. Watermelon's so fat he can hardly move, but he still bites." Keller showed Eli a sickle-shaped scar in the fleshy part of his thumb. "Strawberry looks like she might be a winner, though."

"If they're too fat, then what happens?" Eli asked. Seemed beef cattle couldn't get big enough.

"They can't show."

"You mean you lose your shot at a blue ribbon?"

Keller grabbed at a dried-out cornstalk and broke off

a hollow bit. "Who cares about a ribbon, anyway? If I get one, I'll probably just end up wiping my arse with it." Keller squatted as if he had to go.

"But you never got one," Eli said.

"And neither have you," Keller fired back. "What are they good for, anyhow? My mom's got a bunch and she just stuffs them in the attic. They never see daylight."

Still, Eli wanted a shot at winning one. And he wouldn't do that with his ribbon—stuff it up in the attic and forget about it. He'd keep it in his room, pinned to his bedpost, and look at it every day.

"The good thing is," Keller said, "you can still sell a pig once he's super-fat, even if they get disqualified at the fair. DQ'd pigs make for some good bacon." Keller licked his lips, then put a few fingers in his mouth, plucking them out one by one and making a smacking sound. As if he'd just had a good fill of bacon. "I like mine with plenty of mustard and ketchup. How 'bout you?"

Eli was still thinking about Watermelon as a pig, not bacon. He wondered how Keller could joke about his show animal becoming breakfast.

"Don't the trees look like somebody spilled mustard and ketchup all over them?" It sounded awkward and Eli knew it, but he pointed to the trees anyway, hoping Keller would notice that they did look like fixings.

"You sure see things funny," Keller said. "Like you're not even really a farmer."

They'd reached the old Rupert homestead. A NO TRESPASSING sign hung on the fence outside the vacant property. The pole it was suspended from had been bent to a sharp angle from years of tugging and was overtaken by poison ivy. It jutted out so far, Eli and Keller had to walk into the road to avoid it.

Keller eyed the broken-down barn. Part of the roof had caved in and the lightning rod clamped to its peak was piercing the sky sideways.

"They got a manure machine in there," Keller said. He went up to the barn and peeked through a hole between two boards. "On wheels. It's fun to ride sometimes, when you don't care how you smell."

"You've been inside?"

"All the time. How come you haven't?"

"Well . . ." Eli bent down to make sure his shoelaces were tied. "It doesn't look safe. The roof's caved in."

"Just on one side," Keller was quick to mention. "I'll show you around."

"I don't think so."

"What? Too scared you might get a boo-boo before the fair?"

"No." How could Eli tell Keller that he'd been in enough trouble with Pa already? He didn't want to be going into a no-trespassing barn when he wasn't supposed to, especially one that looked like that.

"The door's around back if you're coming." Keller marched down the path tangled with overgrowth. He cut through bushes of bittersweet with his bare hands and snuck into the entrance.

From outside, Eli could see Keller through a slit in the barn wood. There weren't any stairs, so Keller had stepped on a cinder block to get inside. It had been a milking barn, Eli knew that much. The stanchions hung in the middle, and they looked older than the ones in the Stegners' barn. On either side were empty pens. A trail of broken glass led to the biggest one. Eli was sure it had been the maternity pen. A tin of baby powder rested on its side along the cement floor. But there must've been a fire. The beams were singed. Brittle bits of wood curled up around the edges, waiting to drop.

"Here's the crapper." Keller swung at a rusted-out tub. It hung from the ceiling looking like an oil tank split in two. Keller gave it a shove to send it flying. It teetered a bit but didn't move much. "The pulley's too rusted," he grumbled. He pointed to a whitewashed ladder leading to the hay mow. "Never been up here before."

Keller rattled on the ladder with both fists before starting to climb. A family of turkeys feeding on old corn got scared off. Some of the gobblers were forced to fly through the roof. The rest lurched forward with their fleshy red jowls to get to the other side.

"That's where the roof's caved in," Eli warned from outside the barn.

Keller kept climbing. The next time Eli saw him, Keller had poked his head from the opening and waved.

"Hey, I can see my hogs from up here!" Keller yelled. He turned around and laughed. "You should try. Maybe we'll see—"

There was a rumble and Keller's face disappeared. When Eli finally spotted him, Keller was lying on the cement in the bull pen.

Keller let out a moan. Eli ran as fast as he could to get help.

Chapter Fifteen

❧

Broken Bones

Eli walked to Pa's fields across from the barn, wondering how Keller was doing. Pa'd driven him to the emergency room hours ago and they hadn't come back yet.

The cattle corn was all dried up. It wouldn't be long before it got turned into silage to keep the animals fed all winter. What was taking Pa and Keller so long?

Eli spotted Pa's pumpkin through the gaps in the cornstalks. She sure looked big enough to win the blue ribbon. Wider than a wheelbarrow, her wrinkled bottom rested flat on a pallet waiting to be hauled onto Pa's pickup by the end of the week. That's when they judged the largest vegetables. Tomorrow it was beef cattle and hogs.

Eli did what Keller had done earlier and tore a hollow

bit off a cornstalk. Opening his palm, he expected to find a row of tiny cuts. But there weren't any. Before Little Joe, Eli's hands had been too tender to fend off the prickly stalks; now they were callused up.

Eli took the stalk with him into the barn and got out his show stick. He knew it was silly to think he might still be going to the fair tomorrow. He'd gotten himself into enough trouble already, with Pa finding the lobelia and now Keller falling through the Ruperts' barn. But somehow he had to hold the show stick and poke at something.

He'd been poking at the stalk for a while, taunting it with the tip of his stick, when Pa came in.

"Keller's arm's broke in two places," Pa said. "But he'll be all right."

Eli kept jabbing at the cornstalk, not knowing what to say. How could he ask Pa to go to the fair now? He'd been with Keller when his arm broke. Everyone knew the Ruperts' property was off-limits, but he'd gone on it anyhow.

"Keller told me you didn't go into the barn with him," Pa said. "That's a good thing."

"If you don't want me to go to the fair, Pa, I won't," Eli replied in a hushed tone.

"I want you to."

Eli concentrated on the faded jean creases covering Pa's knees. Had he heard right? He was going to the fair? And Pa wanted him to?

"You worked too hard not to shoot for the blue ribbon." Pa took the show stick that had once been his. "I think you just might get it." Pa twirled the stick around with his fingers before handing it back to Eli.

Eli felt the warmth return to his cheeks as he and Pa walked into the kitchen for supper.

"We're painting piggies on Keller's cast. Wanna help?" asked Hannah.

Keller gave Eli a goofy grin from across the kitchen table. "Your ma already put a row of blue ribbons on the front." Keller smiled. He lifted his baby-blue cast in the air.

"And we spelled *Watermelon* and *Strawberry* on top of them," Hannah added.

"You're still showing at the fair?" Eli couldn't imagine how.

"Why not? It's just a broken arm," Keller said. "I can still carry my show cane. The pigs know what to do anyway. They scoot in the direction I tap their butts with."

"Eli, can you help me drain the spaghetti?" Ma was over the kitchen sink with a steaming pot of pasta. "It's what Keller asked for. Oh, and could you get out the straws, too?"

"What do we need the straws for?" Eli asked. They only used straws for root beer floats or when somebody had a birthday. Somebody who was part of the family. Eli didn't see any root beer on the table. And Keller wasn't family.

"They're to help Keller feed the spaghetti through," Ma explained.

"I can't wait." Hannah giggled. "I've never had spaghetti through a straw before." She'd picked the last crop of daisies from Ma's garden and stuck a pickle jar full of them on the table. "You didn't sign Keller's cast yet," Hannah said, thrusting a tub full of stubby markers at Eli's stomach.

"That's right. You didn't sign my cast yet," Keller teased.

Eli picked out the closest marker in Hannah's container and wrote *Feel Better* near Keller's thumb. But he didn't really mean it. How could they all be fussing over Keller and forgetting about him and Little Joe the night before the fair?

"Should we still put butter on the noodles?" Ma asked. "It might get messy sucking them up with a straw."

"I don't mind." Keller smirked. "I like butter in my face."

Everybody laughed. Except Eli.

"Are you making meatballs, too, Mrs. Stegner?"

"Of course."

"I'll feed him the meatballs," Hannah offered. "I'll cut them up into tiny pieces and make certain they don't touch anything else on the plate."

What was Keller doing here, anyway? Eli was annoyed. And on the night before the fair? There was so much to think about. And to practice in your head. Now Keller was here with his broken arm, about to slurp spaghetti through a straw and messing things up. "Don't your hogs need tending to?" Eli asked.

"They're asleep." Keller snorted, imitating one of his Sour Patch pigs. "Fed them a long time ago. Probably snoring by now."

"Keller's mother's away at a horse show, Eli. He's our guest." Ma placed the steaming mound of spaghetti and a platter of meatballs right in front of Keller. Like he was somebody important or the head of the family. "We're happy to have him as company." Ma rested her palms on Keller's shoulders, just like she did with Eli. "Now he needs a little help eating, Eli, so hand him a straw, please."

Eli tossed a pink straw onto Keller's empty plate.

Keller dangled his good arm next to the chair as if it had gone numb. "Can't do much with this left hand," he said. "Broke the one arm I always use." He took the arm with the cast and angled it closer to the straw, pinching his thumb and pointing finger together like a crab claw.

Eli twirled a few strands of spaghetti around on his fork, not wanting to eat much. He wasn't hungry. He was nervous. What if he forgot how to lead his bull calf around in the ring? What if Little Joe acted up?

"Aren't you the quiet one, Eli," Ma said.

"You're even quieter than Pa," Hannah joked.

"That's because he's thinking about other things," Keller said. He pointed his straw at a noodle and sucked.

"It's a big day for you tomorrow, son." It was the first time Pa had spoken all through dinner.

"And his girlfriend don't like fairs," Keller mumbled through a mouth full of noodles.

"What girlfriend?" Ma asked.

"Tess." Keller grinned. "That's where Eli was before I fell through the barn."

"She's not my girlfriend," Eli muttered, turning beet red.

Hannah pulled a daisy from the pickle jar and started plucking at it. "She loves him. She loves him not. She loves him." A stream of petals collected on the floor. "She loves him not. . . ."

"Stop that!" Eli reached for the daisy stem in Hannah's hand, but she was already on the last petal.

"She loves him. Tess loves Eli! She loves you, Eli! You should be happy."

"That's enough, Hannah," Ma scolded.

Eli wished Keller would leave right now. "Shouldn't you be getting home so your pa won't worry?" Eli stuck his fork into the last meatball on the platter, even though he wasn't hungry.

Keller lowered his chin and lost his silly grin.

"Keller told us if it weren't for you staying outside the

Ruperts' barn, you'd both be waiting for a rescue." Ma sure was treating Keller nice. And now she was cutting up his spaghetti so he could suck up more pieces with his straw.

Didn't anyone care what tomorrow was?

Pa went to sit by the woodstove when supper finally ended and Keller walked home to his pigs. Before Ma finished scrubbing the pots, Pa was snoring louder than Tater. *You'd think it was a regular evening*, Eli thought. Only it wasn't.

Eli put on his chore coat and went to check on Little Joe one more time. He found him by the apple orchard. The cooling night made the calf frisky. He trotted up and down the length of the fence, tail pointing straight out. He stopped and hung over the rail when Eli came near, lifting his head for a pat. Eli climbed through the fence and ran his fingers across Little Joe's back. He felt the silky black coat he'd combed a hundred times, training it to stand up like a carpet.

"You'll behave in that show ring tomorrow, won't you?" Eli whispered into the calf's ear.

But Little Joe was more interested in apples. The Cortlands had turned red, and he swung his neck down to feed. With one forceful sweep of his tongue, Little Joe plopped a lumpy one into his mouth.

Ain't this something, Eli thought. *Little Joe feasting*

on apples, Keller's hogs sound asleep, Pa snoring in his chair by the woodstove in the kitchen. Eli was pretty sure he might not eat or snore again for days.

The moon was full, forming a halo around itself, making the fences whiter and the trees stand out. Eli crawled under the willow tree in front of the house. Its leaves still hung, pale as a honeydew, while the others had been stripped bare. *Nature is funny like that,* Eli thought. That's what Grandpa said. Eli remembered the salamanders' rush to lay eggs, crossing the road for it, then leaving their young to hatch alone. He thought about Fancy and how cow mothers would get themselves all cut up to keep their babies near. Pa'd seen the cycles of nature all his life and he didn't seem to care. Grandpa was a lot older than Pa, but he still saw the wonder of it.

Eli stayed under the willow tree for a long time. When he came inside, the night-light was on in the hall and Ma had hung his show clothes on the dresser mirror. He climbed into bed expecting the katydids to keep him awake, but they were silent. Eli felt certain he was the only living thing in the valley still awake.

Chapter Sixteen

All Jittery

It had been a cold evening. As the dawn broke, a crow cawed. Crows were the only birds who bothered to make noise this late in the season. Fog hovered above the ground while the earth warmed, lifting a little by the time Pa backed up the trailer.

Eli was in the barn with Little Joe, putting a rope halter around the calf's neck. He'd never had the rope halter on this early and gave Eli a dazed look.

"Don't feed him, son," Pa called out from the cab window.

Little Joe tugged at Eli's sleeve, wanting to be fed. "Can't feed you, boy, till we get to the fair." Little Joe sniffed at Eli's pockets. "Didn't have breakfast neither, so we're even."

"Got the ramps in place," Grandpa said, swinging the pen gate open. "I'd say we're about ready. You?"

Eli wasn't sure if he was, but he nodded anyhow.

"Take 'im about six feet back from the taillights." Grandpa uncurled his fingers and fed Little Joe an apple slice. "That's about a cow's length," he whispered to Eli.

Eli guided Little Joe out of the barn and stopped when he was the right distance away. The moon was still up, full and silky like a spotted pig. A few fawns gawked at them from the cornfields, their white spots faded and winter coats already grown.

"Get in the cab, son," Pa told Eli, taking the rope from him.

"What for? I can help."

"Just get in the cab, son. Me and Grandpa will take care of loading."

Eli couldn't see much from the cab's rear window except the silver cone off the trailer's front end. He watched it shift lower and knew Little Joe had gone in. Then Eli heard thrashing. The walls fanning out beyond the metal cone shook from side to side. Eli couldn't figure out if what was happening was good or bad, but it didn't sound very good. He strained to hear Pa or Grandpa, but there were no voices telling him which one it was.

"If he won't go in, he won't go. Don't force him!" Ma shouted from the front porch.

Then Little Joe took off. Eli sure saw that. Running and bucking, with Pa still holding him and Grandpa chasing them both. Out toward the cornfields and into a patch full of needles.

Eli was desperate to get out of the cab, but he knew Pa wouldn't want him to. He scanned the windows for some kind of opening and discovered one an inch wide. "Is Little Joe all right?" he shouted, pinching his face against the glass.

Grandpa nodded. Pa was still on his knees, both pant legs covered in burrs, and the back of his shirt was wet. Grandpa offered Pa a hand, but Pa brushed it aside and got himself up. Then Grandpa and Pa put their arms together and got Little Joe into the trailer.

Pa lingered to make sure the latch was shut tight before getting in the cab next to Eli and driving around the pothole in the middle of the driveway.

"Brought doughnuts," Grandpa said after a while, taking a cardboard box off the dash. "All twelve of them are different."

Pa kept his eyes on the road.

"How 'bout you, Eli?" Grandpa nudged Eli's elbow with the doughnut box. "There's one with sprinkles on it."

Eli didn't think he could eat. The oatmeal Ma had

made before dawn wouldn't go down. And he didn't want to mess up his clothes with chocolate frosting. "I don't want to get any on my shirt."

"You'll get plenty dirty unloading your calf," Pa said, turning into the fairgrounds. "Ma'll bring your show shirt."

Eli took the doughnut with chocolate sprinkles and craned his neck toward the trailer. Little Joe stomped against the metal floor. Eli spotted him poking his muzzle out of a slat on the side of the metal walls.

"We're driving into the show ring," Grandpa announced.

Pa idled the truck underneath a round metal roof.

"Where is everything?" Eli asked. He couldn't tell it was a show ring. More like being parked in a field of sawdust with a roof on it. There weren't even any sides or a particular direction to face.

"They won't roll the bleachers in till this afternoon," Grandpa said. "And hook in the gates right after."

"Go find the stall, Eli. Our name's on it," Pa said. "We'll get the calf weighed in. The show barn's up ahead, where that first trailer's parked." Pa unlocked the cab doors. "And take the chair with you."

Eli hopped into the sawdust with his lawn chair. He eyed the bright yellow sign that said BEEF CATTLE above the show barn. A group of farmers clustered below it, ready to corner an angry steer. "He's got some good brakes on him," the owner joked, letting himself be pulled through the work chute by the restless animal. Eli hoped Little Joe wouldn't need all those men to make sure he got weighed in.

Some older kids were already laying down bedding when Eli walked along the shed row. One was sprinkling, the other forking straw from a wheelbarrow. Eli was surprised that the stalls were just particleboard. He'd never seen the barn before a show, only when it was filled with straw and cattle and people. Eli searched the walls for a taped-up sign with the name Stegner on it. The steel bar of the lawn chair bumped against his ankle each time he moved.

"Coming through!" somebody called out. Eli swung right. "Go left!" the voice boomed. Eli swung left. A bull swaggered by, fully grown and frothing, just like the ones in the *Angus Journal*. The flesh on his brisket rumbled as he moved, commanding attention. His handler stuck out both elbows to give the bull room and gripped the nose chain with thick leather gloves.

Eli stopped and set the lawn chair down for a minute. A father and son hurried past, hauling a show box the size of a refrigerator. *Ma and Hannah will be bringing my show box later*, Eli thought. *When they bring lunch.* Eli tried to stay clear of the middle, where the grooming chutes stood, wheels locked into position with pieces of kindling. A row of soggy cows fidgeted inside them, getting their hair blown out. The kids drying the curly hides had bib numbers pinned to their chests.

"Need help?" one of the groomers asked Eli. She looked down at him and smiled, rattling a can of ShowSheen.

Eli shook his head. So far, he hadn't seen anyone near his age and he wished he knew somebody. "Found it!" Eli cried out, just in case the girl with the can of ShowSheen might hear. He'd found the empty stall with STEGNER written on it. Eli unfolded the lawn chair and placed it beside the post where Little Joe would be tied up.

"First time showing?"

Eli followed the voice up toward the rafters, where a high schooler was balancing on top of a grooming chute. "I'll be down in a minute to show you where to put that chair." Legs straddled, the boy drilled in a sign with his farm's name on it.

Eli didn't remember there being signs. He didn't have one.

"You don't set your chair in the stall next to your show animal," the boy explained, climbing down off the chute. "You put it in the aisle across from him. That's where you and all your stuff goes."

Eli dragged the chair into the aisle, hiding his burning face with a sleeve. This wasn't the same as being at home in the barn with Little Joe, like he thought it might be. He slumped down in the lawn chair and kicked up some saw-dust with the tip of his new boots. How would he keep his calf settled when there was so much to watch out for? There were wheelbarrows to stay clear of and full-grown bulls. Grooming chutes and show boxes as big as appli-ances. And he sure couldn't see a Ferris wheel from this side of the barn. A line of Porta Potties made up the view. Eli hoped Little Joe wouldn't be bothered by it all. Or sense that Eli was.

"Looks like you found the spot," Grandpa said. He got out his jackknife and cut open a bale of straw, sprinkling a portion of it onto the stall floor. "You see that bird up there?" Grandpa pointed at a swallow, darting up to a nest in the rafters. "This is his home and he's all jittery 'cause we're disturbing it."

Eli stared at the bird quivering in its nest.

"But you know what?" Grandpa said. "He'll get used to you. In a few minutes he'll be swooping down to see you like you was old friends."

Eli noticed there were lots of birds above him, all shook up. He got up from his chair, dug into the straw bale with both hands and helped Grandpa spread some over the stall.

"Now go see your pa," Grandpa told him. "He's got your calf in front of the barn, waiting for you to lead."

"Where will you be?" Eli asked.

"I'll be around," Grandpa said, "but out of the way."

Pa was leading Little Joe in circles in front of the show barn. When Eli took over the rope, he could feel the calf tighten a bit, so he started humming. "It's okay, boy," Eli whispered. "You'll get used to it soon enough." Eli kept humming, rubbing his elbow against Little Joe's shoulder as they walked through the barn. They could look each other in the eye now, and Little Joe showed Eli plenty of white.

Pa followed with the alfalfa. "Weighed in at 862," Pa said.

Eli knew that was bigger than most. He tied Little Joe to the post, stroked the back of his neck and smiled. The calf sniffed at the straw for bits of the apple Grandpa had scattered around. Then he snorted at his new neighbor.

The girl was close to Eli's age and barely a finger's length away, feeding her calf Nutter Butters. The little Simmental calf lay on its side, much smaller than Little Joe. His delicate face looked as if it had been whittled out of old barn wood. He shook it every time he wanted another cookie. "How big's your calf?" the girl asked Eli.

"Eight sixty-two," Eli answered. He got out the pitchfork while Little Joe pooped in his new stall.

"Smokey's a lot skinnier," the girl said, looking down at the calf's long brown eyelashes. "And I've already run out of Nutter Butters."

"That don't matter," Eli said. "What you do in the show ring's real important."

"Did you show last year?" she asked.

"No. Did you?"

"No. My sister did. She got the side with the Ferris wheel. You gotta be here a few years before you get the side with the Ferris wheel." The girl looked out at the line of Porta Potties. "Guess we can just climb over to get on our show clothes. The toilet's right there."

They both laughed. Eli picked out some apple slices from the straw to give to the Simmental.

Grandpa and Pa had gotten Eli's show box out of Ma's car and set it down next to Eli's chair. Ma was carrying Eli's show shirt on a hanger, and Hannah held the tub for the water. She dropped it as soon as she saw Little Joe and bounded over to the calf, giving him a great big hug. "You must be hungry," she said, force-feeding him a sprig of alfalfa. "And thirsty, too. I'll get you some water."

Hannah rushed to get the water tub filled from the hose Pa had dragged over. She carried the tub up to Little Joe, spilling most of it onto his nose.

"Stop it, Hannah," Eli shouted. "You'll get him all worked up."

"There's some clean rags in the show box," Ma said.

"I'll open it!" Hannah rushed to the show box before

anyone else. As soon as she unlocked the latches, Spider hopped out.

"There's a cat in here!" somebody shrieked.

Spider darted through the shed row, scattering wood shavings.

"I *love* cats!" the girl with the Simmental exclaimed.

A hay rake tumbled over as Spider nicked it bolting past.

"Hannah, how could you?" Ma cried, chasing after Spider.

The Simmental bucked and kicked at the air as Spider churned up dust when she scooted by.

"Here, Spider!" Ma called. But Spider wouldn't move. She'd found Little Joe.

Tucked safely in between the bull calf's hind legs, Spider sat contentedly and purred. Little Joe snorted, then continued sniffing the straw for apples. Spider stayed between his legs, swirling her tail until he sniffed her, too. Then she moved away and jumped across the shed-row wall and onto Little Joe's back.

"You're as good as DQ'd now," the boy with the drill told Eli.

"Not if the judge doesn't see the cat," the girl carrying the ShowSheen said.

Spider stretched out farther along Little Joe's back onto her white tummy and blinked. Slowly, Eli drew nearer, inching his way toward Little Joe. "Come here, Spider," he said as he beckoned to the cat, extending his arm out gingerly to form a bridge across Little Joe's back. Spider meowed twice, then jumped onto Eli's shoulder.

"You showin' a cat or a cow?" somebody joked as Eli marched to the front of the barn, cradling Spider in his arms so you could see her brown underspots.

Eli hoped he'd be showing a calf.

"I'm so sorry, Eli," Ma said. "If I knew what Hannah was planning . . ."

"I just wanted to make Little Joe feel at home." Hannah sniffled.

Ma took Spider from Eli and curled the cat up in a blanket. "And don't worry about being disqualified. The judge isn't even here yet, so he won't know about Spider. I'll take her home. And Hannah, too."

"Heard your cat nearly got you DQ'd," Keller said. "Good thing you know how to rein her in." He thumped the back of Eli's head with his cast. "Can you help me shave Strawberry? She keeps farting in my face and I show in an hour."

"I can't. I gotta get Little Joe ready," Eli said. He had the show box open, deciding which brush the calf would like best.

"But I can't shave left. It'll only take a few minutes," Keller pleaded.

"Can't you get your pa to help you?" Eli'd seen enough of Keller yesterday. Today was supposed to be just him and Little Joe.

"He dropped me off," Keller began, "but he don't like pigs."

The hog barn was even noisier than the beef barn. Most of the kids ran around chasing their squealing pigs as the animals tried to avoid getting bathed.

"Where's Watermelon?" Eli asked. He stared down at the empty hog pen Keller had led him to.

"Five pounds over. Didn't make it." Keller hopped into another pen with a pink pig in it. "I still got Strawberry," he said, handing Eli a plastic blue shaver. "She needs a shave round her snout. I got this side done." Keller slapped Strawberry on the backside. "I'm just waitin' for her to shift over."

Strawberry peered up at Eli with her round, rubbery snout and grunted. Eli'd never shaved anything before, but the pig looked pretty cut up already. He aimed the shaver at a bristly white hair sprouting out of her chin and stroked it with the blade. Strawberry fluttered her white eyelashes. *Pigs aren't so different from cows*, Eli thought. Just smaller and quicker, but they still liked being stroked and fussed over. "You practice much?" he asked Keller.

"Who, *me*?"

"That's how you win," Eli said.

"I don't win anything." Keller sprinkled the bottle of talcum powder over Strawberry's back and rubbed.

"You never know," Eli said. "Strawberry likes you a lot. You raised her. She'll follow you around."

"They let them loose in the ring and we gotta go find 'em, you know."

"I know."

"I got enough candy in my pocket to keep her close by, though." Keller dug deep into one and brought up a handful of sugar-coated pieces. "Even put some in my boot. That way if I trip, she still won't leave me." Keller smiled. He took the spray bottle and squirted Strawberry's neck with it. "Keep her cool," he told Eli. "She can't sweat."

Keller got out his show cane. "Wish me luck!"

"Luck!" Eli wished back. He started making his way to the beef barn.

"Hey!" Keller shouted. "Know why you never got DQ'd?"

"Why?" Eli hollered back.

"'Cause you got the best-lookin' calf in the barn."

Pa'd already given Little Joe a bath and set him up in the grooming chute when Eli got back. "Get out the blower," he said.

Eli began blowing Little Joe's feet dry, then his tail, working his way up to the neck. When he got to the calf's face, Little Joe licked Eli's nose.

"It's the salt they're after," Pa said, spraying the hairs on Little Joe's topline in place. "Better get your show shirt on." Pa swept up the hairs near the calf's tailhead with a comb, making them stand on end.

Eli rushed to get his checked shirt all buttoned, but his fingers seized up around the last hole. He wondered how he'd be able to work the show stick with his right hand being so shaky.

"Comb out the tail yet?" Pa asked.

Eli took the comb from Pa and stroked Little Joe's tail.

"That's about it," Pa said. He handed Eli the lead strap. "Take him to the gate and wait till they call you in."

Eli couldn't move. The links of metal chain on the lead strap ran cold through his fingers. Anxious show animals sidestepped around him. But he couldn't recall what to do. The lather of sweaty flesh nipped Eli's nostrils. Blowers roared in his ears like tiller mowers. But when he saw Little Joe standing square in front of him, all Eli could remember was how his bull calf looked coming out as a baby, lying small and helpless in a clump on the straw.

Little Joe butted the top of Eli's head with his chin, forcing Eli to do something. Eli gripped the lead strap and guided Little Joe out of the chute and in line by the gate.

He buried his fingers beneath Little Joe's hair and took in the warmth. "I wish I was as calm as you," he murmured, clutching the show stick tighter.

Keep the stick in the left hand when leading, Eli recalled, *and in the right hand to use it.* What else had Grandpa told him? *Turn away from the judge. Or was it turn around for the judge?* Eli was a bucket of nerves. He blinked and eyed the rest of the bulls. The other seven in the class all looked like they could win.

The gate opened. Eli froze. Little Joe led him into the ring.

The bull calf in front of them took a stutter step, pulled back his ears and mooed. The judge's face turned sour.

Eli held his breath, hoping Little Joe wouldn't moo, too. "No mooing," he whispered in Little Joe's ear. But all Little Joe did was kick up some wood shavings and lick his shiny gray nose.

"Line 'em up!" the judge shouted.

Eli watched the girl in front lead her mooing calf. *Keep half a cow's length behind.* Eli'd remembered. He broke away and took Little Joe into the center of the ring, tugging on the chain once the calf's legs were square. Then he switched the show stick to his right hand and rubbed Little Joe's belly with it.

"Your first calf, right, son?" The judge ran a hand across Little Joe's back.

Eli was a bucket of nerves.
He blinked and eyed the rest of the bulls.

Eli nodded and kept stroking Little Joe with the show cane. He could hardly swallow, his mouth was so dry, and his stomach was fisting up, too.

"He's big, boy. What do you feed him?"

"The whole orchard." Eli couldn't help but smile now. "It's where he goes to kick and run." As soon as he'd said it, Eli wished he could take it back—the kicking part. Blue ribbons didn't go to kickers.

"Around the ring once more." The judge made a circular motion in the air with a finger, then scratched his double chin.

Little Joe kept leading, calm as toast. All Eli had to do was follow. The mooing calf jerked up suddenly. Eli and Little Joe were just a few inches back. The crowd rose to their feet and gasped. *Don't do it*, Eli pleaded in his head. *Don't rear back on us.* Quickly, Eli turned Little Joe away, hoping it wasn't too late.

Eli could hear the ring man running, his footsteps grinding down the sawdust, and the girl yanking the lead strap too hard, then crying. But he didn't dare look. *It don't concern you.* Grandpa's voice came back to him. *It's just the judge, you and Little Joe.* Eli rubbed the bottom of Little Joe's cheek with his free thumb. He lined the calf up in the center of the ring, next to an Angus cross with white markings up to both knees. The ring man, half a yard away, twisted up the mooing calf's tail and led him out.

The judge stepped toward Little Joe and pointed to his topline. "Folks, the Angus is a high-carcass breed as you can see."

Did the judge go to third place first or first place first? Eli stood still as a statue, wishing he knew.

"There's plenty of cuttability here in the rib, too." The judge ran his hand down Little Joe's back toward the loin, then below it. "And his hindquarters are longer than most. It may be his first entry, but this young boy and his bull calf are the best in the class."

The judge handed Eli the blue ribbon. Eli felt the silky softness of the prize before sticking it in his back pocket, just like he'd seen others do. Then he led Little Joe out of the ring and tried not to smile too big. Everyone Eli'd competed against patted him on the back and even the ones who didn't.

"You fattened him up just right, son," Pa said. "He's sure to get top dollar at the sale." Pa put a hand on Eli's shoulder, drew him closer and smiled proudly.

It was the first time Eli'd seen Pa smile that way. A well of happiness Eli had never known gushed up and made his ears tingle. He'd pleased Pa that much.

Eli guided Little Joe down the shed row, noticing things he hadn't before. The steady hum of a ceiling fan, cooling a dozing steer. The speckled coat of a tiny calf all glowy from getting a bath. And the smell of manure. He liked the smell of manure. "Told you we'd win the blue ribbon," he whispered to Little Joe, keeping his lips near the calf's ear a bit longer.

When Eli and Little Joe reached their tiny stall, Keller was there.

"Got a spot to hang your ribbon," Keller said, pulling the blue ribbon out of Eli's back pocket. "Right here." Keller had hammered in a nail. He hooked the blue ribbon around it.

"How'd you do?" Eli asked.

"Dropped some candy in the ring by mistake," Keller said. "Strawberry wouldn't stop eating. The judge didn't even get a look at her." He took his show cane by the butt end and tried balancing it in his left palm. It toppled into the straw. "I'm selling her in fifteen minutes at the hog sale," he said. "That's the best part. Getting all that money. Sleeping in tomorrow morning. You'll see."

Keller picked up his cane and walked away. "As soon as she's sold," he yelled back, "I'm getting me a double order of curly fries with gravy."

Eli rummaged through the straw to find Little Joe an apple slice. A sparrow dived down to peck at a chunk but quickly darted up to its nest as soon as Eli stooped over.

"It's a good hour till the sale," Pa said, bringing over a tub of water for Little Joe. "We can walk around the fair for a bit."

Eli waited until he couldn't feel the warmth of Little Joe's breath between his fingers anymore and the calf had dipped down for a drink of water.

He didn't know the sun had been shining. It caught the edges of the Ferris wheel whenever the wind gusted beneath a car and rattled it slightly.

"What do you feel like eating?" Pa kept looking over at Eli and grinning. "I know Ma packed lunch, but you can have whatever you want. You earned it."

Eli eyed a row of candy apples glistening cherry red behind a glass counter and caught a whiff from the fryer at the Bloomin' Onion. He'd imagined for months what it might be like to win the blue ribbon and what he'd do right after. He'd planned on riding the Cliff Hanger. Eli'd figured he might be tall enough to make it through this time. He'd do that first on an empty stomach, then he'd ask Pa about getting an order of elephant ears with cinnamon sugar. Or a waffle ice cream sandwich. Not the skinny ones at the Methodist booth that only cost a dollar—the ones with thick slabs of vanilla ice cream dripping out the middle that cost more.

But now that Eli had won the blue ribbon for real, he

didn't want either. This wasn't supposed to be how it turned out at all. He was supposed to be happy. He'd finally made Pa proud. Pleasing Pa was just about the best thing Eli figured he could ever do. And he'd won the blue ribbon. He'd *really* won it! But he hadn't won it by himself. He'd won it with Little Joe. *His calf.* And in an hour Little Joe wouldn't be his anymore. He'd belong to someone else.

"That's what Hannah likes, ain't it?" Pa pointed to a little glass animal gleaming in the sun at a booth by the grandstand.

"I think so." Eli watched the curly-tipped mane sparkle blue and then pink in the light. *Pa knows about unicorns? He actually noticed one in a line of cluttered glass?*

"How much for that unicorn?" Pa asked the vendor. The glassmaker was snoozing behind the booth and came to, following Pa's fingers to the top row.

"That's a gladiator on a horse," the man grumbled.

"Got any unicorns?" Pa asked.

"You like make-believe creatures, do you? How about a dragon with a long, pointy tail?" The man reached for a dragon by its jagged end.

"It's got a horn coming out of its forehead," Pa explained.

"I know what a unicorn looks like," the man scoffed. "I can make this horse into one," he said, showing Pa a steed rearing up on his hind legs. "But it'll cost you twenty bucks. Horns that long aren't easy to fire. It'll take me two minutes."

"We'll wait," Pa said, handing the man some money.

Maybe Pa noticed more than Eli'd given him credit for. He'd found a tiny stem of lobelia in a fifty-acre field. And he was getting Hannah a gift for no reason. Maybe Pa hadn't forgotten what it was like to raise a calf.

The man put the unicorn on a bed of fluffy cotton and handed the box to Pa.

"I know about Shamrock." There. Eli'd finally said it.

Pa looked as if he'd had the wind knocked out of him. "That was a long time ago," he said. He tucked the box with the unicorn into his breast pocket.

"Not too long," Eli told him. "Grandpa says you never forget your first show animal."

Pa scratched behind his shirt collar.

"So you still remember, Pa? About Shamrock?"

"Some."

"But the hurt's all gone?" Eli stopped and looked up at Pa's face, searching for something they had in common. Searching for any sign of the feelings he had in himself.

Pa reached down, took Eli's hand and squeezed. "Better get back to the show barn," he said. "We don't want to be late for the sale."

Chapter Seventeen

Sold!

Eli tightened his hold on the show halter and pulled Little Joe closer.

"Just make sure to leave his water bucket full."

"Huh?" Eli didn't know what Pa meant.

"Once he's sold, son. Leave water, a bale of hay and you're done. Now let's get this bull calf sold."

Eli blinked at the big blue ribbon Pa'd put on Little Joe's halter, moving whenever Little Joe breathed. He'd done everything right so far, Little Joe had. And Eli'd shown them he had the Stegner touch, too. But Eli wished it was still morning. And there was no blue ribbon. Before Little Joe wouldn't go in. Before Little Joe got so big.

"Now in the ring . . . Eli Stegner and Little Joe, Junior

Champion, bull calf division," the auctioneer hollered. "Eat him or breed him . . . he's the Junior Champion . . . Little Joe."

Eli's shirt collar felt stiff. His new boots weren't even worn in yet, and he felt a blister coming on. But Little Joe didn't look bothered at all as he entered the show ring to be sold.

"Boy, that's some carcass. About a year's worth of barbecuing, I'd imagine!" someone bellowed from the front row.

"Why'd you have to get so big?" Eli whispered, looking at Little Joe from the corner of his eye. "I've got an apple in my pocket," he said. "Why don't you sniff around for it? Rear up or something."

Around and around they walked as the auctioneer cackled out numbers. It was just Eli and Little Joe now, being swallowed up by the lights and the sawdust that smelled like medicine.

Little Joe nudged Eli's arm and tried to lick his hand. "You're supposed to be afraid of me," he told the calf, tugging tighter on the lead chain.

Eli looked up to find something familiar—someone— and caught a flash of white. It came from a belt buckle in the middle row. Eli swung Little Joe away. He knew it was Ned Kinderhoff standing there, bidding on his calf.

Eli took his gaze higher and spotted Grandpa in the

high row, smiling and waving his hat. Eli wished he could feel happy like Grandpa. But he found it hard to breathe and looked down at his boots.

"Sold!" yelled the auctioneer. The crowd gasped at the high number.

Eli felt the blood rush to his ears and block out the noise. He loosened his hold on Little Joe and stood there for a moment with his eyes closed, burning. A drop of sweat trickled down his forehead and onto his upper lip.

"Time to get out of the ring, boy," Eli heard the ring man say. "Time to go."

Grandpa was waiting outside the gate.

"It's all over, Grandpa," Eli murmured, giving him the lead strap.

"I know, son, I know. Now we can go home."

With his hands free, Eli thought about apple season and supposed that Old Gert would get a few extra with Little Joe gone. And he'd have more time for climbing those crooked trees instead of picking them clean. That's how a real farmer would think. A real farmer would be getting curly fries by now with extra gravy.

It was strange letting go and wanting to hold on. Little Joe was still behind him. Eli could feel it. He wanted to look back, but he couldn't. The tears were too close. If he were Fancy, he'd turn around and kick and buck and moo and do just about anything to keep his calf near. But Eli wasn't Fancy; he was a farmer. He wiped his face with his palm. *Don't stop caring just because it hurts*, Grandpa had said. How could he ever stop caring for Little Joe? He could still smell him on his fingers.

"Ready to load up, son?" Grandpa asked.

Eli didn't understand.

"Little Joe's got an apple orchard to eat over at my farm. I'd imagine he's starving."

"But . . ."

"I've been thinking 'bout getting back into it . . . keep the rhythm of life going," Grandpa said. "There's not a young bull finer than Little Joe. He's worth every bit the money I paid for him."

Eli didn't know what to say.

"Now don't think I'm gonna need another one next year," Grandpa added.

"Oh no."

"But Little Joe . . . he's not a bull you want to part with."

"Uh-huh" was all Eli could say. For he'd already grabbed hold of the halter and was feeding the apples in his pocket to Little Joe.

Acknowledgments

Sometimes the best stories come to you in the middle of the night and all you can do is get up and write what you've been told. That's how it was with *Little Joe*. I scribbled down the first few paragraphs, which still stand in their original form, but I needed help with the rest. I found the perfect guides.

First and foremost, Nancy Hinkel, my editor—*Little Joe* would not have become a novel had it not been for Nancy, who read the story in picture-book form and knew it could be more. Associate editor Rebecca Bullene, for her watchful eye on all things ethical, rural, and deeply rooted in the soil. Heather Smith Thomas's book *A Guide to Raising Beef Cattle*, which became my beef bible and a riveting nightly read to this day, along with the *Angus Journal*. Clearfield Farms, run by the Rickards, my Cherry Ridge neighbors, whose chickens, barn cats and newborn Anguses made this story real. Their cattle stared me down in the pasture outside my window each day as I wrote this story. Keith O'Grady, our other neighbor, thank you for seeing the world as you did growing up, and for your bouquets of poison ivy. Ed Pruss, of Penn State's agricultural office in Wayne County, for setting me straight on every question I asked about beef and farming, as did veterinarian Richard Trayes and farmers Beth Troop, Dave Nogan, Jess Scull and Diana Beisner. *Highlights for Children* science editor Andy Boyles, and Mark Baldwin of the Roger Tory Peterson Institute, for making the Big Night chapter come to life. And finally, *Little Joe*'s highest form would not have been achieved without the support of my husband, Rich Wallace, who knew the voice as well as I, and saw that it never faltered. He eagerly read each new chapter and never stopped seeing the wonder of it, making daily walks with me to the cows.

About the Author

After fifteen years as a network TV announcer, Toronto native Sandra Neil Wallace moved to rural Pennsylvania. When she woke up to a mischievous group of runaway Holsteins on her porch twirling pumpkins with their candy-pink tongues, Wallace's curiosity was piqued. A trip to the county fair deepened that interest. Befriending a nine-year-old boy eager to show her his Angus calf, Wallace watched him tearfully flee into the midway after his show animal had been sold. That night she began to write *Little Joe*, her first novel.

Sandra Neil Wallace now lives in New Hampshire with her husband, novelist Rich Wallace, and Lucy, who's a lot like Eli's dog, Tater.